NATHAN'S HEART

MINX MALONE

CrushStar Romance

An Imprint of CrushStar Multimedia LLC

ISBN-13: 978-1-938789-32-8

PRAISE FOR MINX MALONE

One More Day

I am now officially in love with the Alexander family. There was so much about this book that worked for me. First and foremost, I loved the romance between Jackson and Ridley. They had fabulous, explosive chemistry. I loved that Jackson works and lives the music industry. When he sang his song to her, I honestly melted.

--Smitten by Reading (Grade: A-)

Ridley and Jackson explode with passion on the pages of One More Day... this is a pure romance! Ridley and Jackson are a sweet and sensational couple and I can't wait to find out what happens in their future. Malone has a winner with The Alexanders series! Please keep them coming!

--Joyfully Reviewed

The Things I Do for You

“Malone does an exceptional job ... showcasing how two very different people can fall in love.”

--- 4 stars, RT Book Reviews

"Nicholas is perfect leading man material..."

-- 4 stars, Romance Junkies

Ms. Malone does an excellent job of taking an unconventional way of coming together and developed it into a true love story. The sexual chemistry between the hero and heroine was off the charts

--BookKraze Reviews

The book is full of great characters - my favorite had to be Jackson - he is sweet and sexy yet cautious with his heart since he lost his wife in a car accident. The story is well written with plenty of twists... I can't wait to read the next installment of the Alexander brothers.

--Fairy Tale Ending Reviews

Teasing Trent

“I really enjoyed this one...There was a fabulous twist at

the end that I didn't see coming, but it was the absolutely perfect way to end the book. Just fun and sexy!"

--Smitten By Reading

"Trent and Mara have enough chemistry to fuel a rocket ship. Mara's seduction of Trent is classic and hysterical. I mean this guy is out of his depth with this girl but hey the great thing is that he wants her as bad as she wants him. When they finally give in it's explosive! Teasing Trent is hot hot hot!"

--Joyfully Reviewed

The sex between these two is hot! And I must admit I'm thinking about taking up Yoga as a hobby after reading this ;)

--Barnes & Noble Reviewer

CONTENTS

NATHAN'S HEART

I

Evangeline Ford shivered and pulled her thin sweater tighter around her ample chest. The motion only made her girls plump up even more. The guy standing in front of her grinned, revealing a row of crooked, broken teeth.

“Darling, I usually say more than a handful is a waste but I have a feeling I’d enjoy the extra.”

“Do you want to buy a purse or not?” she snapped.

He finally dragged his eyes away from her cleavage and handed her a folded ten-dollar bill. She thrust one of the purses she held into his arms.

"Thanks." After tucking the money carefully in her pocket, she turned to the man standing behind him.

He'd been waiting for a while but she hadn't been able to get rid of her toothy suitor. She only hoped he was a serious customer. If Mimi came back and saw that she'd only sold one purse, she'd never hear the end of it. Evie loved her mother but she wasn't the most responsible person ever. She'd never been able to hold down a job and was constantly following some get-rich-quick scheme. Her latest was selling knockoff purses outside all of the metro stations.

The nation's capitol is filled with tourists, Evie! Most of them don't know the difference between a Coach and a couch so it's the perfect place to sell. You won't have to worry about making rent ever again!

Never mind that the only reason she was so broke was because Mimi had found where she'd hidden last month's rent money and gone on a cocaine and alcohol-fueled bender. They'd already been behind on all their bills so Evie could have just cried at the thought of all that money gone in one weekend. It had happened right after she'd lost her waitressing job and she hadn't found another one yet. Every day things looked worse and worse until their electricity had finally been cut off the day prior.

"Hi, are you interested in a ladies clutch or perhaps a tote?" She smiled brightly at the new customer, hoping he'd buy something out of pity if nothing else.

Despite the bleakness of her current financial state, Evie couldn't believe she was standing out in the cold selling knockoff bags. She didn't even want to know about this "source" that Mimi had found to supply the bags. She planned to just sell and ignore the little voice in the back of her head screaming that this whole situation was bad news.

The guy didn't smile back but just stared at her. After a few awkward moments he finally said, "I need a new wallet. You got any of those?"

She was trying to think of a way to convince him that the coin purse she had could double as a wallet when she saw *him*.

The past few weeks, she'd seen the same guy getting coffee at the shop right across from the metro station. Tall and well-built with dark hair, there was something about him that made her think of a soldier. She could never get close enough to see what color his eyes were but he had a permanent scowl on his face that made him seem pissed at life in general. That wasn't enough to stop him from being the most viscerally sexy man she'd ever seen.

Not that he was the only reason she'd insisted on coming back to this same corner even though she didn't get many people to stop here. Mimi kept telling her she needed to pick a less affluent area but she'd countered that the Foggy Bottom station was used by a lot of students. Students were usually broke, right? But as she watched him swagger down the sidewalk she had to admit a lot of it had to do with getting to see her daily dose of eye candy.

Her customer shifted and cut off her view of tall, dark and cranky. It was just as well. She was supposed to be hustling for rent money not lusting after guys who were way out of her league. Guys who looked like that didn't go for short, plump girls of unknown ethnic origin. Although she'd been called "exotic" before. Whatever that meant.

"I don't have any wallets. But maybe you might want to buy a bag for your girlfriend." She held up the tote bag on her right arm. "This would be perfect for upcoming beach season–"

Her voice dropped out completely when the guy blinked and his pupils morphed into slits. She gulped. He was one of the dragon shifters she'd heard so much about.

"Um, this would be perfect for the beach. Maybe you'd like this one instead?" She tried to play it cool but his smirk told her she hadn't been successful.

Trying not to be obvious she snuck another glance at him. Ever since the dragons had made their existence public, the American media had been fascinated by them. Notoriously reclusive, they claimed to have no ill intentions toward the human population and just wanted to live in peace. She'd heard the stories of course, that they could take out a building with one swipe of their huge claws and the public's fascination had only gotten worse since their king had gone on a late night television show. Handsome and charismatic, the country's female population had become instantly obsessed with the elusive new species living amongst them.

"I'm not a beach kind of guy."

He stepped closer and her breath automatically sped up. She'd heard the rumors about them snatching girls but she'd figured she was safe. No one snatched big girls. Maybe this was just a dragon thing, like the imposing height and the creepy eyes.

"A clutch, maybe?" Her voice came out as a squeak.

The dragon shifter took a long inhale. "No, I already know what I want."

Then he smiled.

As Nathan Drake dodged another streak of lightning, this one so close he felt the heat, he had to acknowledge that there was a lot he'd do for money. But this shit right here...

He swerved again as thunder crashed to his left, the reverb vibrating through his wings. Fire left his throat on a bark of displeasure. It wasn't easy to correct course while carrying a two hundred pound crate but his client had made it clear that every one of his shipments needed to be delivered within an hour of pickup.

The arrogant way his former king had ordered him to take the job had been almost enough for him to ignore the elegant missive that had arrived by personal courier six weeks ago. But he'd decided to take the job and not just for the considerable purse, although a hundred grand per delivery wasn't anything to sneeze at. More than that, he wanted what Avan dangled in front of him like the most precious of jewels. Safety. Security. The promise of an ally in the event his clan ever needed one.

The thought of an alliance with the dragon he hated most in the world had filled him with rage but in that moment, he'd thought of his father. His last memory was of the light leaving his eyes but he had years and years of memories before that, of a man both steadfast and wise. As clearly as if he'd been right there clapping him on the back, he'd heard his father's last words.

Take care of your brothers.

If it was just about him he'd tell Avan exactly where he could stick it but the safety of his clan had to come first. So he'd taken the strange job despite all Avan's warnings about how important his deliveries were. He'd insisted that each pickup take place on a Friday at five o'clock in the afternoon and reach the Rivenell stronghold in precisely one hour. Flying from D.C. to the mountains of the neighboring state of Virginia was hardly difficult and he'd delivered each week's cargo with no issues.

But not in the middle of a fucking monsoon.

Another bolt of lightning whizzed by but this time the flash of energy caught him in the wing.

"Damn it!"

At least that was what he said in his head but all that came out was an anguished roar of pain. His right wing burned like hell but he struggled to keep it extended. He'd never reneged on a job or delivered late but this storm was worse than expected. It was time to accept defeat.

Either that or end up losing a limb.

Nathan executed a gentle turn, keeping a firm grasp on the harness in his talons holding his cargo. Luckily it was only a medium-sized crate so he could still move quickly enough to dodge the random flashes of lightning streaking through the sky. He'd only been flying for ten minutes so it made sense to just turn around and take shelter in his own den. His land was pretty close to his current position just outside of D.C.

He pumped his wings harder, using the turbulent wind to propel him faster. Five minutes later, the land he inhabited with his brothers came into view. Circling several times, he dropped the crate gently in front of the entrance to his den and then shifted mid-air. He landed on his feet with a thud. Shaking off the impact, he immediately turned around and sprinted back to his den. His dragon didn't mind getting wet but his human side didn't appreciate it.

He hefted the crate in his arms and carried it inside. He glanced around the room and then made a split-second decision to keep it in his bedroom. He and his brothers had been couriers for some expensive shit before. There was no telling the value of what was in this particular crate, especially considering how adamant the king had been about receiving it on time.

Fucking Avan.

It still irked him that he'd been forced into this job in the first place. But no one said no to the dragon king. And he'd been tempted when he got the king's letter.

It had been a powerful message, not just the words on the page but the jarring realization that Avan had always known where they were. The dragon sitting on *his* throne and leading *his* people had sent him a letter as if he was summoning any underling to do his bidding. Nathan ground his jaw as he deposited the crate in the corner of his room.

He may not be a true king, not according to the old laws, but he'd managed to lead his small clan to both safety and prosperity. His brothers all worked with him and together they'd built their business until they were the most sought after recovery specialists in the world. In the beginning they'd used their natural dragon-born instincts to ferret out treasure and to recover a few things they shouldn't have, selling a cadre of jewels, artwork and precious metals to the highest bidder. Now that they were on their feet they could afford to turn down jobs that seemed too risky. Although he kind of enjoyed some of the more dangerous missions.

His heartbeat increased suddenly and the damn thing felt like it was banging against his ribcage. Then came the heat. Nathan staggered, propping a hand on the wall to keep him from falling on his ass. Damn, mating fever. Flying expended so much energy that he'd taken the job knowing he wouldn't have any trouble ignoring the fever. But in his human skin, it was going to be a bitch to fight off. Maybe he could shift and ride out the worst of it.

He glanced toward the front of his den. The two windows in the front, the only ones in the place, showed that the storm hadn't lessened any. As a dragon he stood about twenty feet high so the only room in his den where he would fit was the living area and he wouldn't be able to move much. What he needed was a good hard workout.

Or a good, hard fuck, he thought bitterly. But since his last girlfriend hadn't been cool with how often he was away, he didn't have anyone to help him with the lust currently trying to burn through his system.

"Good hard workout it is."

He changed into running shorts, a t-shirt and sneakers. Then he grabbed his boxing gloves from his dresser and tapped the speed dial on his phone to call his brother. He put the phone on speaker so he could tape his hands while they talked. Although maybe shedding a little blood would help him calm down.

"What's up, Nate? Aren't you supposed to be on your way to see the king? Tell me you didn't drop it."

He made a face at the phone. "Of course, I didn't drop it. My perfect record is still intact."

Both of his brothers had dropped or damaged cargo at least once before. He hadn't yet and they loved to remind him that the day was coming.

"So what's going on?"

"The storm. I couldn't keep going. I almost lost a wing as it was."

"Shit. Avan is going to lose it when he finds out. He was

extremely clear that he expects prompt delivery and no questions every time."

Nathan really wanted to say that Avan could go fuck himself but he figured there was no use taking his frustration out on Ian. His brother got enough shit dealing with their demanding, intractable customers.

"I know. But I didn't have a choice. Just wanted to give you a heads up so you can avoid him when he calls. He probably won't realize there's an issue for another hour. I've got his crate right here in my room. It's perfectly safe. I'm sure whatever it is, his lord and master can wait until tomorrow morning to get it."

Ian sighed. "Fine. I'll try to stall him. But I'm pretty sure he's going to find a way to take this out of our hides."

His brother hung up without waiting for a response so Nathan tossed his phone on the bed. He walked down to the gym on the other side of his den and spent an hour pounding on the heavy bag. Afterward, he stripped the clothes from his body so he could shower. The warm water didn't soothe him the way it usually did. By the time he got out he was just as antsy as before. Back in his room, he pulled on a pair of worn-in jeans and just as he was pulling a t-shirt over his head, he heard it. A soft shuffling sound.

A second later his scales came out. Only purebred dragons descended from the royal line could shift partially. It was a handy skill in situations where he wasn't sure if there was a threat. The iridescent gold scales shimmered in the semi-darkness as he moved through the room closer to the crate. Then he heard it again. A shuffle. Then a soft whimper.

"Oh no."

Frantically, he started pulling at the boards holding the crate together. Their company refused to carry live cargo but it didn't stop people from trying to break the rules. It was just like Avan to ask him to pick up some exotic pet and with his luck he'd have to figure out how to feed and water a tiger cub or some exotic monkey.

He yanked at the last board and then pulled back layers of padding covering the contents. At first his mind couldn't reconcile what he was seeing, it just sent him random information. Arms, legs, long dark hair. His mouth fell open. Avan wasn't trafficking exotic pets.

It was a girl.

2

Evie's first thought was that absolutely everything on her body hurt. She opened her mouth to moan but got a mouthful of something scratchy. Coughing weakly, she tried to move her arms to push whatever it was away but found she couldn't do that either. The muscles in her arms and legs screamed as she attempted to stretch out.

"Oh god, help." Her voice was so soft that she almost couldn't hear herself but the slight sound was enough to send her into a spasm of pain.

"Don't worry, I'm going to get you out of there. Just hold on."

The unfamiliar voice sent terror through her once more.

Who was that? It wasn't a voice that she'd ever heard before. She winced at the sound of cracking wood and curled into herself. The last thing she remembered was … what? Her brain felt scrambled and it was hard to think beyond the pounding in her skull but she vaguely remembered Mimi fussing at her before she left their apartment. Had she been robbed? But who would want to steal the crappy knockoff bags she was selling?

As it was she couldn't even give the damn things away.

"Okay. Can you move?"

The deep voice rumbled somewhere above her so she tentatively opened one eye. It was dark and she couldn't see much other than the huge form hovering over her.

"What happened to me?"

The large form moved again and the pressure against her side was removed. She let out a tortured groan when her legs shifted. It shouldn't hurt this much to move her limbs.

"I have no idea sweetheart but I'm going to find out. What's your name?"

She hesitated. Should she really be talking to this man she didn't know? For all she knew he was the one who'd done this to her. Then she thought that maybe if she was cooperative he wouldn't hurt her. Especially since she wasn't in any kind of shape to defend herself like this.

"Evie. I mean, Evangeline Ford. Who are you?"

"Nathan Drake. Come on, let's get you out of this box."

Tentatively, she stretched out her legs. They were sore but she could move them. She planted a hand beneath her torso and pushed up.

"Slowly. Careful now." He put his arms under her and then stood with her clasped to his chest. That's when she became aware that she was completely naked.

In too much pain to even be mortified, she clung to him weakly as he turned and placed her gently on something soft. A second later, a soft light turned on bathing them in a warm glow. She looked up and then instantly froze.

"It's you!"

"Do we know each other, sweetheart? Because I'm pretty sure I'd remember."

There was a slight southern twang to his words that coupled with his deep, rumbly voice sent a wave of warmth though her veins. And other places. She clenched her thighs together, embarrassed that she could get turned on even when she was all beat up and sore.

He glanced down and then looked away sharply. His jaw clenched and then he pulled his shirt over his head. "Here, put this on."

His bare chest was so perfectly chiseled that Evie was momentarily stunned. Tall and lean, there wasn't an ounce of fat on him anywhere. His six or was it eight, pack led down into two V-shaped muscles that took her eyes places she didn't want to be caught staring.

She yanked the shirt over her head, glad to have something to do other than gape at him. It was tight on her which was embarrassing enough but it also molded to her breasts in such a way that her nipples stuck out like headlights. Headlights on high beam. Great.

He ran a hand over his head, sending his dark hair into disarray. "That didn't help as much as I thought it would."

"Sorry." Her cheeks burned as he made himself busy looking at everything but her. "They're not so easy to cover up."

He glanced at her again. "Yeah, I can see that."

An image of him, scowling as he walked down the sidewalk, flashed through her mind. That morning!

"Oh my god. You were there this morning. I remember!"

Evie gasped and scuttled backward on the bed. The movement made her head pound again and she clasped her hands on her temples, as if she could hold the pain in.

"Whoa. Take it easy." He held his hands up and approached slowly. "Why don't you tell me the last thing you remember?"

"I saw you getting coffee at Java Hut and then this guy was pretending to be interested in the bags I was selling. He must have done something to me. Drugged me or something."

She started to tell him the guy was a dragon but something stopped her. What if he was one of them, too? She peered at him closely, waiting to see if his eyes would change or if he'd suddenly grow a tail. Hell, she'd only seen pictures or video of dragon shifters before today and they'd always looked a little creepy to her. Not like this guy.

His dark hair was cropped close and his eyes were a deep brown. Bedroom eyes. He looked more like an underwear model than anything else. She flushed when he caught her looking.

"I don't really remember anything other than that."

He looked like he didn't believe her but thankfully he didn't push. "Well, I *was* at Java Hut this morning. I always get coffee there when I have a job in the area."

She scoffed. "What job? Abducting people?"

To her annoyance, he didn't look at all upset about her accusations. Instead he chuckled and crossed his arms, the impressive muscles in his arms bulging in that position. She turned her head away, refusing to be swayed by his unbelievable hotness. This was obviously their plan. The creepy one did the dirty work and then they brought in a hot human guy to convince you to let your guard down. Well, no way. Not happening.

"I didn't do anything but pick up a crate for delivery. I'm a courier."

"You just carry stuff and have no idea what it is? I'm supposed to believe that?"

He shrugged. "Believe what you want. It's not my job to worry about what's in the boxes. I'll carry whatever as long as I get paid."

"Mercenary."

"Necessary," he countered. "My brothers call me Heartless but they don't know how many times my lack of scruples has been the only thing keeping food on the table. Heart is a luxury of the rich."

"I know." Evie's anger deflated somewhat. It was hard to judge his mercenary approach to life when she knew all about the compromises you'd make when you were hungry.

"Speaking of getting paid, I guess I won't be since I get paid on delivery. And obviously no one was supposed to know what was in this particular delivery. This is going to be a problem."

Evie's mouth fell open. She'd been assaulted and kidnapped and all he was thinking of was his lost paycheck? *Bastard.*

"It's slightly more of a problem on my end, don't you think?"

He smirked. "I just meant that since I was never supposed to know what was in the crate, it's going to be problem when I don't show up to deliver it. Actually, the only reason I came home instead of going straight to the drop-off point was because the storm was so bad. Lightning probably saved your life."

Evie shivered. He was a jerk but he was right. She could be waking up in an entirely different situation right about now. It was terrifying to think of how close she'd come to being another statistic. All at once, she wanted nothing more than to go back to what was familiar. To see Mimi and their crappy apartmcnt and her own bed.

"I want to go home," she sobbed.

His eyes darkened with an emotion Evie couldn't even begin to identify. "I can't do that, sweetheart."

"Why not? Just let me go and no one has to know. You could pretend you lost the crate or that I escaped." She put her hand on his arm, momentarily distracted by the sensation of warm skin stretched over hard muscle. "*Please.*"

The shock on his face mirrored how she felt inside. Mortified she snatched her hand back. It had seemed like such a natural instinct to touch him. To appeal to his sense of goodness. Even though his part in her abduction had been accidental, he readily admitted that he only cared about getting paid. He called himself *Heartless* and somehow she still thought he was good?

It was official. She was the worst hostage ever.

She touched me.

The thought rolled around and around in Nate's brain as he paced the room. Evie watched him from the bed, worried. *She should be worried*, he thought grimly. She was far too beautiful with that honey-tinted skin and those big brown eyes. Her touch had set off a firestorm inside of his body, the warmth from her small fingers quickly igniting every nerve ending from his arm straight to his groin.

It was like walking with a stick of dynamite in his pants. He tried to adjust discreetly when she wasn't looking but the friction of his jeans moving across his cock only made it worse. He bit off a curse as the damn thing pulsed so hard he was afraid it would go off in his pants. He hadn't been that green since he was a teenager.

"Okay, I want you to tell me everything you remember about what happened earlier."

He swiped a hand over his brow. Maybe if he focused on the task at hand instead of her taut little nipples poking against the front of his shirt, he'd have a chance to calm down.

"There was a man. He had crooked teeth and his eyes ..."

Now that got his attention. He crossed his arms and waited until she met his gaze. "What about his eyes?"

"Um, they were dragon eyes," she finally whispered. She looked away and tugged the shirt down a little lower.

He groaned. "That is not good news. I was hoping this was some kind of mistake. That maybe you were in the wrong place at the wrong time or the crate somehow got switched with another one. But if you saw him..."

"Why? What does that mean?" She moved forward slightly on the bed and her intoxicating scent washed over him again.

"It means we're in deep shit. I have no love for the dragons but I would have never expected this."

Heat washed over him again, so intensely that it stole his voice. He staggered backward and placed his palms against the wall. His vision started to dim as his blood raged and burned. He pushed with all of his strength, hoping he could channel the intense energy into something, anything other than doing what he really wanted to do.

Marching over to that bed and burying himself in all the curvy softness he knew was hidden beneath his t-shirt.

"Are you okay? Nathan?" She said his name hesitantly, as if unsure of how it would sound in her mouth.

He wanted to tell her to say it again, wanted to hear it in that honeyed voice or better yet hear her scream it while he was making her come. The image appeared in his mind so vividly that his hands curled into fists against the wall to prevent him from turning around and grabbing her.

When her hand landed on his back, he let out an anguished roar, not unlike the sounds he made in dragon form. Lost in his internal torment, he must not have heard her when she got up. But as much as her touch made him burn, it released a wave of relief so intense it almost brought him to his knees.

Startled, she pulled her hand back. "I'm s-sorry. I didn't mean to–"

As soon as her hand left his skin, the fire came back. The desire that had previously been at bay returned with a vengeance.

"Put it back! Your hand."

His words came out in a grunt but she quickly complied, her small hand resting tentatively in the middle of his back. The soft moan he let out would have been embarrassing under any other circumstance but he didn't care. His world was reduced to his bare skin and her gentle touch.

"Are you sick?"

She stroked over his shoulder blade, rubbing a gentle circle over the feverish skin. All he could do was hang on and absorb her touch. Nothing had ever felt like this.

"No. I rarely get ill."

She was accelerating his fever but she was calming it too. That could only mean one thing. *Fuck.*

"You're sweating and your skin is all red. Maybe you should rest. I promise I won't tell anyone what happened. Just let me go and no one has to know."

Nate crossed his arms as tightly as he could. Not that it would stop him from grabbing her if the fever took over.

"I can't do that. It's freezing out there and it's the middle of a lightning storm."

She shivered then, wrapping her arms around her middle. "I guess that's true. If it's this cold in here I can't even imagine being outside in this."

Everything inside of him stilled at her words.

She's cold. Our woman needs our warmth. His dragon instincts ignited and in that moment his entire worldview narrowed to one purpose only. Making sure Evie had whatever she needed.

He scooped her up, ignoring her startled gasp and carried her to the bed. Moving the comforter back with one swipe of his hand, he placed her in the center of the bed.

"What are you doing?"

He slid in next to her and her mouth dropped open. "You're getting in, too?"

"You're cold. I need to warm you."

She worked her mouth but no sound came out. Then finally, she let out a small laugh. "I could sleep on the couch."

"I can't let you sleep out there. You would be alone. Undefended. You're vulnerable when you sleep."

Tired of conversation that wasn't accomplishing his goal,

he wrapped his arms around her, molding her against his chest. Just the idea that she would sleep out of his sight made him crazy. Nathan knew he was being irrational but something about this girl fired his protective instincts.

Considering they were going to be stuck inside for a while, that was a problem.

3

Evie tried to play it cool and act like a drop dead gorgeous man wanted to snuggle her on a regular basis. Inside though, she was freaking out. Currently she was plastered against about six feet five inches of muscle and it all felt rock hard.

Rock. Hard.

"So this man you saw earlier, can you tell me anything else about him? Had you ever seen him before? Following you, maybe?"

His voice rumbled against her ear and she suppressed a little shiver of delight.

"I don't know. It all happened so fast."

"Try. Anything you can remember might be helpful. Maybe he hung out in the area?"

Evie thought back but honestly she probably wouldn't remember if she did. She wasn't the most observant person in the world, something that Mimi chided her for on a regular basis. It was just so easy to get lost in her daydreams, especially when there were no customers. Her mind worked in images so she was usually imagining what colors and textures she'd use on her next art piece. It had gotten her into trouble more than once when she'd wandered into the wrong part of town because she wasn't paying attention or bumped into someone because she wasn't looking where she was going.

It was hard to pay attention to real life when her imagination was so endlessly entertaining.

"He was taller than I am, I know that. Older, some gray hair."

"What about his eyes?"

She tried to shift away slightly but his arm tightened around her waist like a steel band. She sighed.

"I already told you. They were dragon eyes."

He made a frustrated sound, the warm huff of his breath

against her ear sending a stab of desire right between her legs. She clamped her thighs together, hoping he wouldn't know why she was squirming. It would be just her luck that he'd know exactly how turned on she was just from him whispering in her ear.

"Okay, he's a dragon but did he have dark eyes or light eyes before they changed? Crows feet, long eyelashes, hell. I thought women were supposed to notice those kinds of details."

She grinned despite herself. "Normally we do but not when the guy is creepy. But I think they were brown."

"Okay. So tell me everything you remember. Start from the beginning and maybe more details will come back to you."

Evie tried to calm her mind. Somehow he seemed to know what she needed because he nuzzled the back of her neck.

"Relax sweetheart. Just talk to me."

Inexplicably, his words worked like a balm to her system and she found herself telling him everything. About the crappy apartment she and Mimi struggled to pay rent on each month, to the crazy plans her mother was always coming up with to make money. Even though he didn't say anything the whole time, just listened in that quiet intense way of his, he made her feel like he understood and didn't judge her.

"Who is the male in your life?" he asked finally. "Why does he not provide for you?"

It was such a strange question that Evie momentarily forgot her situation. A male? He had a strange way of speaking, almost like he was much older than he appeared.

"I, um... don't have a male."

"What about your father? Your family?"

"It's just me and Mimi. My mother," she clarified. "It's always been just the two of us. I've never met my dad."

She didn't tell him that she didn't think Mimi knew who her father was. When she was young, her mother had claimed he was in the Army and died overseas. As she'd gotten older and asked more questions it became obvious that her mother was keeping the truth from her. Knowing what she did of her mother's habits now, Evie figured it was more likely that Mimi didn't remember the night she was conceived. Or she remembered and wished she didn't.

Some things were better left unknown.

"Say what you will about the dragons but this would never happen in a dragon clan," Nathan grumbled. "There you would be protected and cherished. Females are a rare treasure because they are so few."

"That doesn't make sense. How do they, you know?"

"What?"

Evie rolled her eyes. No doubt he knew what she was asking but just wanted to force her to say it out loud. "If they don't have many dragon females, where do the dragon babies come from then?"

She looked over her shoulder and their faces were so close that their lips brushed slightly. He closed his eyes slightly as if pained. *Of course, he doesn't want me perving all on him,* she thought. *He looks like a Crossfit ad and I'm just... me.*

She tried to move back and put some room between them but his arm clamped even tighter, pulling her against his chest so closely that her breasts rubbed up against his chest. She sucked in a startled gasp when her sensitive nipples brushed against him.

"Most of their mates are human," he said finally.

She pushed back from him and he was so startled, he actually let her go.

"*Oh my god*, the stories are true then? They really snatch girls and steal them from their families? Is that your job, huh? Get close to girls, they trust you because you're human and then you abduct them?"

His face twisted. "No. That's not true and no dragon would want to gain a mate that way. In their culture, if a male can't prove himself worthy of a mate, then he doesn't deserve one. That is their way. It would be a great dishonor to your family and your entire clan to do something like that."

"I guess the guy who did this to me didn't have much honor."

"The man who did this to you is dead once I figure out who he is." His voice was fierce and the murderous look on his face convinced her that he meant it. Maybe he really wasn't involved.

"I'm sorry I accused you. This whole thing has been pretty crazy." She blew out a breath.

"Don't apologize to me." He sounded almost angry. "Anyone would be freaked out by what happened to you."

It was strangely comforting to see his anger on her behalf. Evie was used to fighting her own battles and up until this moment would have sworn she preferred it that way. But there was no denying that having a sexy man who looked like he wanted to kill to protect you was ... intriguing.

"Well, at least I got to see a dragon up close. He was scary but his eyes were such a pretty gold color."

His face twisted and suddenly his expression was nothing short of terrifying. "His eyes were gold? I thought you said his eyes were brown?"

"At first they were brown. But when they changed, the slits were gold."

"Fuck." He sat up suddenly, the change in position taking her off guard.

Evie wrapped her arms around her middle, cold again for reasons that had nothing to do with the temperature in the room. "Why? What does that mean?"

"Only members of a certain family have gold eyes with very few exceptions. It's been that way for centuries. I don't know exactly who did this to you but I know who he's working for."

She didn't know anything about dragon shifters so why

would anyone be targeting her? If they were hoping to ransom her, they wouldn't have gotten far anyway. With the way Mimi tended to disappear when she was in search of a fix, there wouldn't even be anyone to send the ransom note to.

Which was kind of depressing.

"Why would anyone target me? It's not like I have any money."

"Money isn't what he wants," Nathan said gravely.

"Who?"

"Avan. The Dragon King."

She moved forward slightly on the bed and the intoxicating scent that was uniquely hers swirled between them. His eyes drifted closed, enjoying it before he realized what was happening.

No.

He couldn't let his guard down around her at all. Otherwise he'd have her on her back in the middle of his bed.

"This is a little hard to believe. The king is after me? That guy doesn't seem like the type who needs to kidnap women. He could probably just stand on the corner and crook his finger and have a harem if he wanted one."

He made a face. "Yeah, whatever."

"Oh, come on. Those eyes are a little weird but he's still pretty hot." Her eyes softened when she said it, like she was imagining the man in question. She licked her lips.

His dragon didn't like that at all.

"He's an asshole," Nathan ground out. "And his... *hotness* aside, it's entirely likely that he's behind this. It's not common knowledge but the dragon king is not well. He's older and still without a mate. A dragon too long without a mate is at risk of dissolution."

"Dissolution? What does that mean?"

Nathan struggled to think of human terms to explain. Humans didn't have an animal nature so it was probably a foreign concept to them of losing their grasp on their humanity.

"It means the dragon in question starts to sink further into their animal instincts. Eventually you lose your higher functioning completely. You become more animal than human."

It wasn't until after he'd said it that he realized she might wonder how he knew so much about it. Luckily she didn't seem to catch his slip. She was watching him closely, her eyes trained on his mouth.

Then she licked her lips again.

"Um, let me get you something else to wear and then find an extra blanket. I'll take the couch so you can have the bed."

"Okay. But first, can I have something to drink? I'm so thirsty."

"Of course. I should have offered you something."

He left the room and walked down the hall to his small kitchen. When he'd built his den, it hadn't occurred to him that he'd ever need more than the basics so the setup was functional more than attractive. He pulled down a glass from the cabinet next to the sink and filled it with water.

You don't even know how to treat a female. Giving her water from the tap? This isn't worthy of her tongue.

He suppressed the inner rumblings of his dragon and

carried the water carefully back down the hall. Evie accepted it with a small smile that soothed the beast a bit. Until she proceeded to drain the glass in one sitting.

When she finished, she swiped her arm across her mouth. "That's what roofies do to you. Makes you feel just as dry as a bone."

"How would you possibly know that?"

She gave him a sardonic look. "It's not the first time I've been drugged. Plenty of girls learn the hard way not to leave their drinks unattended."

Anger flowed through him. He couldn't take the images rolling through his brain just then. Pictures of Evie vulnerable and alone. Of some nameless, faceless male taking advantage of her when he wasn't there to protect her.

"What's wrong with your face?"

He looked up to see that she'd recoiled from him. His fingers touched his cheek tentatively. The scales that had come out without his knowledge felt smooth under his touch. He turned around so she wouldn't see. After taking a deep breath, he felt them flatten back out.

"Nothing for you to worry about. I'm going to keep you safe. That's all you need to know."

"Okay." She didn't sound convinced and he wasn't either.

Already he craved the sound of her voice. His body reacted to it like a drug that he'd been deprived of for too long. How the hell was he going to keep her safe when he couldn't even control his body's reaction to her?

Well, you're going to have to.

He lectured himself as he left the room and then grabbed the extra blanket from the hall closet. His phone vibrated in his pocket and he pulled it out. "What's up, Ian?"

"You don't want to know. Kavan called asking about the package. Apparently he's the Regent's Second now."

"Really? Interesting. Little Kavi did well for himself. I wonder what Jovan thinks of that." Nate chuckled at the thought of his hot-headed cousin being usurped for the Second position in favor of his younger brother.

Ian grunted. "Jovan was always unpredictable. Too unpredictable to act as the King's right hand. Anyway, I knew Kavi wouldn't be happy but when I told him you were delayed due to the weather, well, saying he lost his shit is severely understating the issue. We have to deliver that package or I think he's going to send out enforcers to take it. What the hell could be that valuable?"

Nathan turned and his eyes locked with Evie's. Still sitting on the bed, she crossed and uncrossed her legs before tugging on the bottom of his shirt. Her nipples still stood out against the material. To his shock, she rubbed her palms over the tight points, as if trying to relieve an ache.

"Just stall him. I'll think of something."

He hung up and then moved closer to the room. Evie's eyes remained on his the entire time.

"Evie? Are you okay?"

She bit her lip and the innocent act sent most of the blood that wasn't already in his dick in that direction.

"I don't feel good. It's just really hot in here or something."

She tugged at the end of the shirt again. Then crossed her legs again, letting out a small moan when her thighs rubbed together, like the friction of her own skin against skin was unbearable. Nathan understood the feeling because that was how he felt, too. In an instant he understood what was happening.

"It's affecting you, too."

Her brow furrowed and he didn't even bother explaining. He dropped the extra blanket on the bed and then strode out of the room. Through the living room and out the front door, he kept going until his jeans were soaked through.

But after standing in the rain for a few minutes, he had to acknowledge that he was in deep shit. Because apparently he wasn't the only one affected by the mating fever.

Evie was feeling it, too.

4

Evie clenched her jaw and tried to think of anything but how uncomfortable she was. It had started as just a faint ache between her thighs and then came the heat. A rush of warmth that rolled through her bringing a flush to her cheeks and a tight knot of... *something*... in the pit of her stomach.

After shifting around on the bed for a while, she'd finally decided to stretch out. Nate had been outside for a really long time now and she wasn't sure what the hell he was doing. It appeared that he was just standing in the rain but she couldn't really tell. The guy was weird, there was no denying that but after spending so much time working for the secretive dragons, what else could she expect?

Or maybe he just wants to get away from you.

Her shoulders slumped at the thought that he'd rather stand out in the freezing rain than have to talk to her any longer.

Not the most comforting possibility when he stood between her and freedom.

Another throb of warmth unfurled from her belly and this time it was so strong, she curled in on herself forming a little ball on the bed. Her entire world shrank to that one sensation of heat and light and need. She needed something and only one man could give it to her. She cried out, a mournful sound and then just like that, he was there.

"I've got you, sweetheart. Just hold on to me."

Evie sobbed as she clung to his damp chest, the scent of his skin all at once the most comforting thing in the world. This man that she'd never even seen up close until today was suddenly the center of all that was good and right in her world. He was the only one that could calm this storm raging inside. It didn't make any sense but when he anchored his strong arms around her, she knew for sure that she didn't care. As long as he didn't let go.

"Stay with me. Nathan."

She whispered his name, embarrassed at how needy she sounded. How could she want him so much when they'd only just met? But to her relief, he didn't rebuff her or push her away. He seemed to know exactly what she was craving.

"I think, under the circumstances, that you should call me Nate." His deep chuckle ignited another curl of sensation in her core.

"Nate." She whispered his name, wondering why it felt so right.

He turned her in his arms so her back was pressed against his chest and then buried his face in her hair. Tingles of sensation spread throughout her at the intimate contact and it brought tears to her eyes.

"What's wrong with me? Why do I feel like this?"

When he answered, his lips moved against her skin and it felt so good she seized in his arms. He held her throughout the spasm, petting her arms gently, bringing her down from the violence of her reaction to a place of gentle warmth.

"Evie. There are some things that are happening... Fuck. I

don't even know how to explain. But I need to keep you close to me."

She nodded even though she didn't really understand. "Okay."

It should have been awkward, resting in the arms of a man she didn't even know. But somehow, Evie felt like she could rest and let go of her troubles for the first time in ages. She let out a soft sigh and sank deeper into the embrace. The next thing she knew, she woke to an empty bed.

She sat up slowly pushing her wild curls out of her face. It was completely dark except from the light coming from the open door. Her legs and arms were still sore, something she realized as soon as she started moving around. *Take it slow.* Stretching out first one leg, then the other, Evie stood gingerly and stretched.

"Nate?" She called out his name tentatively. There was no response.

Her heart rate picked up. Had he left her here alone? She stepped out into the hallway and looked up and down the dark corridor. Maybe this was some kind of test and he wanted to see what she would do if she was alone. But she didn't even get the sense there was anyone else in the house.

This was her chance.

Loneliness blanketed her and she was suddenly, inexplicably sad. When Nate had held her and comforted her, she'd been content in a way that she'd never experienced. Even though she knew logically what she needed to do, there was no denying that her emotions were pulling her in the opposite direction. Her traitorous, silly heart wanted her to stay curled up in his bed waiting for him. To let him hold her close again and protect and love her.

Can you say Stockholm syndrome? Snap out of it, Evie!

Looking down at the shirt that barely covered her ass, she wished that she had been kidnapped while at least wearing pants. But she might not get another chance like this. It was pretty much now or never. The stone floor was cold under her feet as she walked to the front door. It wasn't locked and she tugged on it, wincing as it creaked when it opened.

She emerged into the night on a wide, grassy field. It was still raining lightly. She looked behind her. Nate's house appeared to be built right into the ground somehow. You'd miss it if you didn't know it was there. There were several other houses in the distance that looked similar.

She chose a direction at random and started walking. Hopefully she'd hit a main road and could find someone willing to call the police on her behalf. Mimi probably hadn't even realized she was missing yet. It was a scary thought, the idea that no one knew where she was. What was her life worth if she could be kidnapped and no one even noticed? It was like she was completely invisible, screaming at the top of her lungs but not making a sound.

Nate would notice, her stupid silly heart whispered.

Even if Nate seemed nice, the truth was there were way too many holes in his story. There was something going on with him and history had taught her that when a man was evasive, he was hiding something.

"Hey! Who are you?"

She spun around, her bare feet slipping slightly in the muddy grass. A man stood a few feet behind her glaring at her. He was good-looking and tall with dark blond hair. He was also *pissed*.

"I'm lost. I was just looking for the road."

She thought that sounded like a completely plausible story but his face twisted in disbelief.

"Nice try. There are no roads anywhere near here. How the hell did you find us? Who sent you?"

Stunned by his angry manner, she turned and ran in the other direction. There was a strange crackling sound behind her and she glanced over her shoulder. Her mouth fell open but no sound came out.

In the field behind her, the man was gone and a huge gold dragon stood watching her. He flapped his wings and flew over her, landing in the field on the other side cutting off her only avenue of escape. Evie screamed as the force of the wind generated by his massive wings hit her like a wave.

She dropped to her knees and instinctively covered her head.

"Evie!"

Nate's voice, colored with fear and anger, sounded behind her. Even though she was pretty sure he was a criminal who may or may not have kidnapped her, she didn't want him to get eaten by a monster. She managed to stumble to her feet then and ran back toward him.

"Run, Nate!"

He was obviously either really brave or really stupid because he kept running in her direction. She looked back at the huge dragon now advancing slowly behind her, looking even scarier the closer he got. Evie whimpered when he roared, emitting a long stream of fire that came so close she felt the heat on her face. Running faster, she ducked as something whizzed over her head.

Confused, she looked around for Nate but he was gone. Maybe he'd taken her advice and run back to the house. When she finally reached the threshold of his door, she looked behind her and gaped.

There were now two dragons flying overhead. Streams of fire burst from both of them but then one of them flew away. The other circled in the air, flying lower and lower. Then the huge body shimmered and shrank into itself and Nate landed on his feet directly in front of her, completely nude. He blinked at her with gold-slitted eyes.

Evie fainted.

Nate cursed as Evie's eyes crossed and she fell back against the door. Luckily, he managed to catch her before she banged her head against the frame. Her head lolled against his shoulder, her dark hair cascading over her face.

Damn Ian, he thought.

His brother was just as vigilant about their security as he was but for the first time ever, he wished his brother was a little less zealous. What the hell had he been thinking, shedding skin in front of an obviously helpless human female?

They'd had reporters, groupies and dragon hunters search them out before so they were constantly vigilant about protecting their privacy and the location of their clan. But Evie was clearly not carrying any kind of weapon or even a camera. Where the hell would she put it? She wasn't even wearing proper clothes.

Another thing that sent his blood pressure skyrocketing.

His dragon definitely didn't like that his brother had gotten a good eyeful of her lush breasts straining against his shirt and the creamy smooth skin of her exposed thighs. A rumble emitted from his throat at the thought of any other man viewing her soft curves and Evie stirred in his arms.

Calm down, asshole. She's not ours.

He placed her gently on the bed, pulling the comforter over her again. It was his own fault for leaving to talk to Gavin while she was asleep. His youngest brother had a bad habit of ignoring his phone so both Nate and Ian knew to go bang on the door of his den if they really needed him. He spent the majority of his time absorbed in his books.

No one knew what he was researching or why but Gavin spent every spare second he wasn't working collecting, reading and analyzing the old dragon texts. Maybe he was looking for a cure for the mating fever. Nate could only hope there might be a way out of being a slave to their biology but he wasn't holding his breath.

"You're one of them?" Evie's soft whisper startled him.

He sat on the edge of the bed next to her. She pulled the blanket up higher, shielding herself from him. After the closeness they'd shared earlier, her withdrawal cut straight with all the deadly precision of a knife.

He closed his eyes. "Yes. I am."

There was a soft shuffle but Nate didn't dare look. If she

was glaring at him with reproach or worse, fear, he didn't want to see it. He wanted to remember her the way she'd been earlier, pliant and warm in his arms. Looking at him like she'd trust him to protect her from anything.

He grabbed his phone from the dresser and texted Ian. *She's not a reporter. She's with me. I should have warned you I had a human here.*

After a few minutes he got a terse response. *It's cool. What are we going to do about Avan's delivery. Do you want me to take it?*

Nate gritted his teeth. *Tell him I dropped it. If he wants to come here and take what doesn't exist, let him try.*

He immediately turned his phone off, not wanting to see how much shit his brother would give him over that.

"You're never going to let me go, are you?"

His head lifted at the soft question. Evie watched him with quiet dignity, not making a sound despite the tears on her cheeks.

Without a word, he plucked her up and deposited her in his lap, blanket and all. Keeping his distance became impossible when confronted with her distress. It was impossible for any dragon male not to comfort his mate when she was in need.

Mate?

He rejected the thought. That was nothing but the mating fever talking. He'd been way too long without a female. But either way, it was too deeply ingrained to protect women for him not to react to the sight of a woman crying. His dragon rumbled in his chest approvingly as she clung to his bare chest, her tears dampening his skin. He whispered to her softly, not even aware of what he said. In that moment he would have promised her anything to take that fear from her sweet face.

"It's all going to be fine. I would never harm you and I promise I'll get you home safely. Just not right now."

She glanced up at him, the tears on her cheeks making a silvery trail against the soft honey shade of her skin. "Because of the weather? I don't care if it's raining. I just want to go home. My mom is going to be looking for me."

She said the last part defiantly and Nate got the sense that the opposite was actually true. Was she all alone in the world? Who was there to protect and care for her?

"It's not just the rain. Evie, the men who did this to you are powerful. And they're still out there."

Her eyes widened slightly before she nodded. "What are we going to do?"

"My brothers and I will handle it. But I don't want you to worry about any of that. Nobody will get to you here."

He became aware all at once that her face was pressed against his neck. She brushed her nose back and forth against his skin, then inhaled deeply. His cock stirred, desire snaking through his veins with every soft touch.

"You smell so good. I just want to taste..." Her tongue against his skin sent fire racing over every inch of his skin.

"Evie, you don't know what you're doing." He tried to disentangle them but her arms locked behind his head, pulling him down on top of her when she fell back on the bed.

"Yes, I do."

"No, you really don't. Dragons go through an extremely fertile period. I never realized our Mating Fever could affect humans so strongly but I think that's what's happening."

"Fever? Yes, that's what it feels like. Ever since I saw you a few weeks ago, your face is the one I see when I'm alone at night wishing for someone to hold me."

Nate could barely breathe since her long legs were now wrapped around his waist holding him firmly in the cradle of her soft thighs. The words penetrated in a slow drip. *A few weeks ago? Alone at night?*

"You thought about me?"

"Yes."

She breathed the words on a soft sigh that made him think of all the other decadent ways he could coax that sound from her lips.

His dragon rumbled triumphantly as the words took shape and meaning. If she'd been feeling this way for weeks, then her attraction to him wasn't because of the mating fever. It was because she truly wanted him. The knowledge thrilled and spurred him. He looked down at her face. She looked like an angel with her long lashes resting gently against her cheeks and her full lips set into a small pout. He finally did what he'd been trying to hold off on for so long.

He kissed her.

As her taste flowed through him, his dragon roared blasting him with the truth he could no longer deny. Evie affected him so strongly because she was his mate, his heart, his reason for existing.

My treasure. Mi tesarik.

His dragon instincts clamored at him to take her, satisfy her and spread her open to take his seed. His human side struggled for the composure to take things slow and not scare her. The thought of her being afraid calmed him enough to keep him from flipping her on her stomach and sinking deep with no delay.

Need to take our mate. Bind her to us. Claim her.

He took a deep breath and buried his face in her neck. She smelled so sweet that his fangs itched to descend and bite her. But he wouldn't mate her until she understood what that meant. First he had to woo her gently and make her love him.

Take her now. Claim her now!

Nate ignored his dragon screaming for total domination but he wasn't able to stop his hands settling on her hips in a rough, possessive grip. Evie moaned at the pressure and rolled her hips.

Fuck.

His lips covered hers completely, dominating her and forcing her to open for his possession. She whimpered beneath him and locked her legs behind his waist, pulling him closer.

Her enthusiastic response only fueled his desire, stoking the flames higher and higher and sealing her fate.

She wasn't leaving this bed until he'd shown her what it meant to be loved by a dragon.

5

"I was drawn to you the first time I saw you. Just the sight of you, the smallest glimpse would stay with me all day. And all night."

Evie felt like she was watching herself from afar, hearing the words pouring from her as if observing something happening in a movie. The tiny rational part of her brain was screaming at her to shut up.

Why are you telling him these things? You don't really know him.

The part of her governed by her heart shoved rational Evie into a mental closet and locked the door. Emotions she'd never experienced stormed her defenses, leaving her raw and ravaged. It was such a scary thing but for some reason, she was calm. A sense of rightness settled over her as he cradled her closer. When their bodies met, everything that had ever been wrong in her universe ceased to exist.

All she cared about was him.

"You dreamed about me?" His deep voice, colored by wonder, weaved through her senses.

There was something hypnotic about it, compelling her to spill what was in her heart, making her feel even more tightly bound to him. She couldn't have lied to him in that moment even if she'd wanted to.

"You were what kept me going when I was cold or hungry or just tired. I need you, Nate."

Her confession hung between them and her breath stuttered in her chest as she waited for his response. His eyes drifted closed briefly but then he looked up at her directly.

"I need you, too. You don't even know how much. *Mi tesarik.*"

His lips slanted over hers, the kiss more like a reclamation than a caress as he held her so tightly she could barely breathe.

My treasure.

The word echoed through her head and somehow she knew that was what he'd meant. It was a truth that she didn't even question. She was his to take, to pleasure and to cherish. It was something she knew with certainty.

Suddenly she was clawing at his shoulders, trying to hold him tighter. She needed him inside of her, showing her what it meant to be truly wanted. At her touch, he growled.

The deep, sexy noise aroused her instantly and Evie squeezed her eyes shut, ashamed at how wet she was just from the sound.

"Open your eyes. Never hide from me."

His voice was different and Evie instantly obeyed. Brilliant gold-slitted pupils gazed back at her. She was no longer with just Nate. His dragon wanted her, too.

"Yes, I see you understand. You are my mate, the reason I exist. My dragon is very possessive of what's his."

His eyes lowered to take in her breasts straining against his shirt. The sight of her curves confined seemed to enrage him.

"Your beauty should never be hidden." He pulled at the bottom of the material until it ripped clean up the middle.

"Oh wow, I could have just taken it off."

Evie cried out loudly when his lips latched onto one of her nipples. Those magnificent gold eyes stayed on her the whole time as he rolled the stiff tip between his lips. He bit down slightly harder than she was expecting but the bite of pain sent a sharp jolt of pleasure through her.

"Yes, just like that," she whispered.

He continued down, kissing over the skin of her belly before he stopped and then bumped her clit with his nose. He closed his eyes. "Your scent is magic."

Evie gulped, unprepared for the intense way he was staring at her most intimate place. Most of the guys she'd been with had treated foreplay as something they had to do. No one had ever looked like they wanted to dive in before.

"I want your fingers," he growled.

Stunned, she held out her hand automatically. He drew her fingers into his mouth, sucking deeply until her fingers were thoroughly wet. Then he tugged them lower.

"Put your fingers on your clit. I need my tongue deep inside you. I need your taste."

“What? I don’t–“

Her eyes practically rolled into the back of her head when he licked her pussy roughly a few times. Need coiled deep in her belly and her fingers started a slow, awkward rhythm. With every stroke of his tongue deeper and deeper, her fingers swirled and rubbed until the tight coil of need snapped and left her shuddering amidst a storm of emotions.

She barely registered him sitting back until he pushed her thighs wide open. Evie blinked through her tears. God, he was *watching* her. Sitting there watching her pussy as it clenched from the aftershocks of the most intense orgasm she’d ever experienced. The intensely possessive way he watched her pleasure, like he was internalizing it, caused another shiver.

His eyes lifted to hers. “You’re my mate, Evie. Do you know what that means?”

Unable to speak, she shook her head. He crawled over her, his eyes on hers the whole time. Their lips met in a gentle kiss.

“It means this is mine.” His fingers curled into her, pushing deep. “It means *you are mine*.”

His fingers plunged again and Evie moaned as another orgasm threatened. Nate looked down and she did too, watching as he took his fingers from her body and used her moisture to coat the length of his cock. She shivered anew as he stroked himself to his full length. He was beautifully shaped, long and thick, and her muscles clenched again at the thought of taking all that inside. Of being possessed by him completely.

"It means you're my treasure. My heart. *Mi tesarik.*"

He whispered soft words that didn't make any sense to her. She recognized that he must be speaking another language but it all just rolled over her, she was so drugged by the pleasure still running through her veins. Suddenly it was all too much and she clung to him weakly, needing something, anything to stop the ache.

"I need you, Nate. Need you."

A low growl permeated the air between them. "I know what you need, my heart. Me."

He settled himself between her thighs, his hips spreading her thighs wide. She was so wet that when he entered her, she took all of him in one thrust. Her back bowed and her mouth fell open at the shocking pleasure of being so filled with him.

"You're so beautiful. So perfect."

He flexed his hips again, sliding through her sensitive folds to notch against a spot deep inside that made everything go dark. Evie wrapped her legs around him, the change in angle keeping him right where she needed him. She bit her lip as pleasure ripped through her again but this time he didn't give her any time to recover. Just kept rocking against her, pushing through her clenching muscles to hit that same magic spot over and over.

"Fuck, Evie. You're so tight." He threw his head back and growled as he came, the muscles and veins in his neck standing out in stark relief.

Evie watched him, greedily taking in the sight of him in the throes of his own release. It was so deeply satisfying to know that she had done that. He sighed and then looked down to where they were joined. She followed his gaze to where he was buried between her thighs. Her eyes drifted closed and she succumbed to another rolling wave of orgasm, triggered by the sight of him rooted deep.

A wave of fatigue followed, dragging her into that place between asleep and awake. Nate lowered himself slowly until his face was in the crook of her neck and rested there, just breathing her in. Content to stay where she was, she curled her arms around his neck and held him close. She wasn't sure how long they stayed like that but jolted awake when he pulled out of her gently.

Panic rose up from her core, clawing at her insides as he climbed from the bed. What the hell was wrong with her? Just the thought of him being out of her sight made her shiver.

"Please don't leave." It embarrassed her as soon as she said it but it would have taken more strength than she had to keep it in.

"I'm not leaving, *mi tesarik*. I just want to clean us up and then make you something to eat. I need to feed you. What would you like?"

Relief made her feel light as air. "I'll eat whatever. I don't need anything fancy. You know, whatever you have handy."

He shifted from foot to foot, suddenly looking so bashful that she had to smile. "I don't really have anything you can eat here. When I'm hungry, I go hunting."

It was such a strange thought to imagine him hunting something down and probably eating it raw. After being so close to him, it was a startling reminder that he wasn't human. Not even close. As if he could read her mind, he lifted her chin gently with the tip of his finger.

"I may look like you, Evie, but I'm not. I'm a predator through and through. My dragon kept you in bed so long because he likes the thought of keeping my seed in you."

Evie blushed. "Your dragon sounds like a Neanderthal. Does that mean he plans to keep me chained to the bed as his sex slave?"

Nate didn't answer. He kissed her gently, the soft brush of his lips against hers sending a rush of warmth though her. When he finally lifted his head, his eyes were almost sad.

"You should have run faster."

After cleaning them both up with a warm washcloth, Nate left his mate curled up content in his bed. There were several missed calls on his phone but he wasn't in any shape to deal with the outside world right then.

His concern and entire focus was on the woman who'd suddenly become his entire existence. Every step away from her had been a struggle. Even now, his dragon pushed him to hurry through gathering food so they could get back to her.

It was an unfamiliar feeling, this urgency, but he found it didn't make him feel tethered or confined as he'd always assumed it would. Instead he felt... complete.

Nate yanked open the refrigerator and then the freezer. The food situation wasn't as dire as he'd assumed. There were still a few microwave dinners from the last time Jonas, Gavin's apprentice, had gone shopping for him. He would have preferred to hunt something for her and cook it himself but there was no time for that.

At the insistent knock on his door, his scales came out. He walked back to his room and then pulled out a pair of jeans from his dresser.

Evie watched him curiously. "Are you going out?"

He leaned over and kissed her. "Someone is here. No matter what you hear, don't come out. No matter what, do you understand?"

She nodded quickly. He hated the worried look on her face, so he kissed her again.

"Don't worry. It's probably one of my brothers. But even if it isn't, I would defend you to the death. You know that?"

Her eyes softened. "I know."

The knock sounded again. This time it was followed by Ian's impatient, "Nate, open the damn door already. I know you're in there."

His relief that it was only his brother was short-lived since he was hiding a pretty big secret from him. It wasn't that he thought Ian would try to give Evie over to the king but every time he thought about telling him, his dragon went crazy. He couldn't handle the idea of any risk to his mate, no matter how remote.

"I'll be back."

He pulled the bedroom door closed behind him. His brother would be able to smell her on him. There was no hiding the scent of sex, especially not to a dragon's sensitive nose. But Ian could be very single-minded and if he was coming to bitch at him about the botched delivery, he probably wouldn't worry much about the girl in his brother's bed.

It was a good thing Gavin was always tucked away in his den because fooling his intuitive and extremely observant youngest brother wouldn't be so easy.

Nate pulled open the door to a very wet, very pissed off,

Ian. Then his brother shifted to the side and he saw Gavin standing behind him.

Shit.

Ian pushed past him. "What the hell took you so long?" Then he stopped and took a deep inhale. He pinned Nate with a hard look. "Tell me you haven't been blowing off my calls because you're too busy boning that chick?"

"Fine, I won't tell you."

Gavin came in and closed the door behind him with an apologetic smile for Nate. "Sorry to intrude."

He waved away the apology. "I know how he gets."

Ian grunted. "*He* is trying to keep our clan from war. I told Kavan that you never checked in and that I believe you might have been injured in the storm. It's strange though."

"What's strange?" Nate asked.

"He kept asking me all of these questions. I don't think he believed me."

Ian paced back and forth between the kitchen and the living room. Every time he got close to the hall leading to the bedroom, Nate tensed.

Other males are near our mate. They will try to take her from us.

His dragon screamed for him to put his body physically between the other two males and his mate, who lay unsuspecting and vulnerable a few feet away. She was so much weaker and had no scales to protect herself. Even though it was just his brothers and intellectually he knew they would never try to take a female he'd claimed, his dragon didn't like their scents being in the same space she was.

Gavin leaned against the wall near the kitchen, looking like he'd rather be anywhere else. He was also much closer to the bedroom than Nate would have liked. Why couldn't they sit in the living room like civilized creatures, anyway?

Pain in his hands drew his attention and he looked down to see blood dripping from his closed fists. His talons had come out unconsciously. It took quite a bit of effort to force them to retract. The gouges in his palms started healing instantly.

When he looked up, Gavin was watching him.

"What's up with you? Every time Ian moves toward the hall you look like you want to go for his throat."

Caught, Nate folded his arms. He hadn't been planning to

hide his mate from his kin but it was harder than he'd expected to tell his brother, who'd lost his *tesarik* so young, that he'd found his mate.

"I wasn't answering your calls because something happened. I found my mate."

Ian stopped pacing. "The woman in the field. She's the one."

Nate nodded.

Gavin came forward and clapped him on the shoulder. "What do you need from us?"

Humbled, Nate closed his eyes. Even in the midst of his own pain, his brother's first thought was how to help him.

"I want our land secure and this thing with Avan handled. I won't bring her into danger." He glanced at Gavin. "I never knew how it would feel when I found her. How do you do it? How do you breathe without her?"

Gavin coughed and looked away. "Sometimes I don't think I've taken a deep breath since that day."

He didn't need to elaborate. They all knew what day he meant, the day their father had been exposed as a traitor to the clan, stripped of his crown and they'd been cast out.

The day Gavin's young mate had perished in the ensuing battle.

After a long moment, Gavin clapped him on the shoulder again. "Don't worry. I'm so close to finding a way to break the mate bond. Soon we won't have to be tortured like this. We'll be free."

Something clenched inside of Nate at the thought of severing his bond with Evie. Just a day ago he wouldn't have believed it but he didn't want to break the mate bond. He would die a thousand times before contemplating life without her.

As his brother was forced to do each day.

He looked at his little brother with new eyes. Nate couldn't even fathom a day without his heart but Gavin had been heartsick for years over his dead mate. He pulled his brother into a hug. Gavin stiffened at first, unprepared for the show of affection. Then he relaxed into the embrace and exhaled, a sound filled with years of grief.

"I hope you find it, brother. For your sake more than mine." Nate murmured.

Gavin held on tighter, like his brother's strength was the only thing keeping him upright. "For all of us."

6

When Evie woke the next morning, it was to a broad muscular male chest and the sound of snoring. It was so unfamiliar but strangely endearing at the same time that she buried her face back in her pillow and just took in the moment. She was tangled up with a sexy man. She was warm. She was safe. She'd been woken several times in the night to a talented tongue on various parts of her body.

In her world, it honestly didn't get too much better than that.

Her happiness dimmed slightly at the thought that while she was warm and safe with her dragon protector, her mother was probably hungry and alone in their dark apartment. Evie pulled the covers over her head, nowhere near ready to face reality. Unfortunately her conscience wasn't easy to escape.

Would Mimi even be able to make a proper meal from what was in the pantry? Since their electricity had been cut off for a few days, everything in the refrigerator was a loss but there were crackers, cereal and some canned soups that she could heat up on the gas stove. But her mom wasn't likely to remember that if she was high. Evie usually had to force her to eat at all when she was strung out.

She hated it, having to force her mom to cooperate and feeling like she was enabling her bad behavior. But after so many years of taking care of Mimi, she didn't know any other way to be. Her mother's bad decisions had long ago become part of the landscape of her life.

Was it any wonder that she wasn't too sad that Nate was keeping her away from home? Shame battled with happiness. It had been so long since she'd been responsible for her mother that she didn't know what it was like to just live for herself. To let someone else take the reins. Not in the way Nate wanted to take care of her, anyway. Was it really so bad that she wanted to stay here in the fairytale for a little longer?

I'm a horrible person, she thought.

"What are you thinking about, my heart?" Nate's deep voice rumbled against her ear just before his arm curled around her waist, pulling her against his body.

"Just wondering if my mother is okay."

"Call her. You can use my phone." He leaned over the edge of the bed and when he came up, he handed her his phone. She held it steady while he unlocked it. It was silly but she couldn't deny it was a thrill when he didn't try to hide the code from her.

Mimi answered after three rings. "Who is this?"

"Hey, it's Evie."

A soft squeal came over the line. "Where have you been, sweet pea? I was worried when you didn't come home."

"I'm sorry I worried you. I'm okay. I'm... with a friend."

Next to her, Nate watched her with a quiet intensity. Already she felt like they were so attuned emotionally that she could tell he wasn't pleased at being referred to as a "friend". But she couldn't imagine telling her mother that she was now mated to a dragon shifter that she'd known for less than a day.

Although truthfully that wouldn't be any stranger than the things her mother normally said to her.

"That's good. Finally having fun for once. Is he handsome?"

She glanced over at Nate and bit her lip. "Yes, he is. Very handsome."

His eyes darkened and in the space of one blink to the next, the gold-slitted pupils she loved made an appearance. She'd noticed his eyes changed when he was either aroused or angry.

"Well, this is a surprise. When do I get to meet him?"

"Tonight," Nate rumbled. Evie's mouth dropped open. *Really*, she mouthed. He nodded.

"I heard that," Mimi chirped. "He even sounds handsome. Well done, chickie."

Evie rolled her eyes. "Anyway, I guess I'll see you tonight."

"Oh, what about the bags? Did you sell any?"

"Just one. But don't worry about that, okay? We'll figure out another way to get the rent money."

She had no idea how they would but after what happened

to her, there was no way she was going to stand outside alone and sell anything ever again.

"Listen, Mimi. Stay away from that metro stop, okay? You were right about it being a waste. Besides, there were some guys hassling me there."

"I hope you kicked them in the balls. That's what I would have done."

"*Mimi*, promise me you'll stay away!"

She'd assumed that she was safe from being snatched but look what had happened. Her mom was still a beautiful woman, despite the ravages the drugs had taken on her body. She hoped Mimi would listen to her for once.

"Okay, whatever you say. I've had decent luck down near the mall so I'll keep working that area. There are always lots of tourists there."

"Good. Okay, I'll see you tonight. I love you, Mom."

When Mimi answered, she sounded pleasantly surprised. "I love you too, Evie. You're a good girl. Always were."

After she hung up, Nate tossed the phone back on the floor. Before he could ask her any questions, she buried her face back in the pillow.

"Can we stay in bed for a little while?"

"Of course. Come here." He wrapped his arms around her and rested his chin on top of her head.

She could sense his confusion but luckily he didn't question her. It wasn't like she knew how to explain what she was feeling. What rational person could understand or explain the things that had happened over the past day? She'd been kidnapped, ravished by a dragon and was now happily cuddled up with him. None of it made any damn sense.

Nate claimed she was his mate but what did that even mean? It was so tempting to believe him and trust that he would take care of her but that just wasn't the way things worked in her world.

He'd probably get tired of her soon and then her life would go back to the way it was. How serious could he really be about a girl he'd known for only twenty-four hours? It felt so disloyal to wish that she didn't have to go back but this whole thing felt like a moment outside of time.

Was it really so wrong to enjoy it while it lasted?

O*ur mate is unhappy.*

Emotions had a flavor, something Nate could never have imagined before he'd found his other half. But he could feel her emotions through their bond, her essence present in the back of his mind like a part of his own personality. He could feel that she was scared and hurt.

Our mate cries.

His dragon was disturbed not just that their mate was upset but that she wasn't telling him why. How could he protect her when she didn't confide in him?

Once her heartbeat slowed, he pushed her gently to her back. He leaned over her, his arms caging her in. "Why did you not tell me you needed money?"

Her mouth fell open. "Why would I tell you that? It's not your problem."

"Anything that affects my mate is my problem. I would not have you worrying about lodging or how to pay for it. It's unacceptable."

Evie's eyes dropped to his mouth then she started giggling.

"I'm going to start calling that your alpha dragon voice, when you get all deep and growly."

He wasn't sure what that meant but was glad to feel the sadness that had been cloaking her lift. "I do not understand your humor."

"I know." She grinned up at him. "But it's funny to me when you get all intense and dragon-y on me."

He grunted. "My mate should not be worried about anything. I will take care of you."

"It's the twenty-first century, Nate. I can take care of myself. Even though I haven't been doing such a great job lately. But that's because I got too comfortable."

"What does that mean?"

She sighed. "My mother has a lot of problems. I learned a long time ago that I have to hide money from her or she'll spend it. She found my hiding place last month. It was particularly bad timing since I had just lost my job."

"Your mother needs help? We have to go to her."

Immediately he got up and pulled on the jeans crumpled on the floor. She pulled the covers up to shield her bare breasts, a move that made him scowl.

"Now? Are you even allowed to fly in broad daylight?"

Nate chuckled. "I would love to see a human government try to tell a dragon when he's *allowed* to do anything."

"Fair point. So I'm not going to have to get back in a box or anything, right?"

A smile tugged at the edges of his lips. "No, my heart. You are one of the lucky few who will get to ride a dragon."

Joy suffused her features, then the sadness returned. He resolved to figure out what was bothering her before the night was through. But that would have to wait. If his mate's mother needed help, they needed to provide it. He may have been kicked out of his clan but he'd managed to create a new one with the same values and ethics. They took family seriously.

She stood at his urging and he rummaged through his dresser to find a shirt and pair of sweatpants for her. He rolled the sweatpants at the waist and cuffed the legs. It was still way too big but it would do until they reached her den and she could gather her things. She didn't have shoes either so he gave her the thickest pair of socks he owned. Hell, maybe he'd just carry her the whole way.

"Nate?"

He looked up to find her watching him contemplatively. Then she stood on her toes and kissed his cheek.

"Thank you."

"For what?" Nate shifted, caught off guard by how her sweet affection made him feel.

"I don't know. Just everything. Listening to me vent. Wanting to help my mother. All of it."

"With time you'll understand what it means to be a dragon's mate. It means that I'm privileged to care for you. And that includes the people you love. We are forever bound."

"Forever isn't something I'm familiar with. I'm used to *until I get tired of you*. But thank you for wanting to take care of me. For however long it lasts." Evie's eyes glowed with gratitude.

Nate reminded himself that she was human and didn't understand their ways. She had no way to know that he didn't want her gratitude for taking care of her. It was his duty and privilege to show his mate what it meant to be cherished. He tugged on a wayward curl before tucking it behind her ear.

"I think with time you will understand how dragons define forever. But until then, just know that I can feel these things that trouble you and I will always try to comfort you. I don't want you to have to worry about anything."

"There will always be something to worry about. If it's not the money, it'll be something else. If I can get kidnapped in plain view, I don't think I'll ever feel safe anywhere again."

"I can protect you." He concentrated until his scales came out, the gold shimmering even in the low light.

Evie gasped. "What is that? The same thing happened before when your brothers came."

He rotated his arm so she could see the scales move and shift. "Scales. I can shift partially if I need to protect myself. I can even breathe fire in my human form. These are things only descendants of the royal line can do."

"They're so beautiful. May I?" She held up her hand and he nodded to indicate that she could touch him.

He tensed, unsure how it would feel to be touched while his scales were out. But like every other experience with his mate, it was beyond compare. Her touch awakened nerve endings he didn't know he had. *I've just discovered a new erogenous zone*, he thought. But most important, his mate now knew his claims to be able to protect her were legitimate.

"No one will hurt you again. Ever. I will protect you with my life."

She stroked over his scales once more, then enveloped him in a hug. "I believe you."

7

Evie had never experienced anything as thrilling as flying. Nate had insisted that she ride inside of a special harness that essentially strapped her to his back. It hadn't been the most comfortable thing ever but once they were airborne, it had ceased to matter. Soaring through the air on the back of the man she loved, she'd felt completely free.

Even though he was technically allowed to fly whenever he wanted, he'd explained that he preferred to avoid human scrutiny whenever possible. Because of that, they would be landing on the roof of a building owned by a fellow dragon shifter.

As soon as Nate landed, Evie unhooked her harness and scrambled off his back. He folded in his giant wings and then a heartbeat later Nate stood before her, chest heaving.

For as long as she lived, Evie didn't think she'd ever get used to watching him shift from dragon to man or back again. It happened so seamlessly that she could watch it again and again and still not understand how he did it. She also appreciated watching him pull the clothes they'd brought along over his truly extraordinary naked body. If his heated looks were any indication, he was happy to show off for her.

"Don't get cocky, Mr. Dragon. This stuff isn't so impressive, you know. Plenty of guys have a nice ride and a rocking hot body."

"I'll take your word for it." He winked at her and then folded the harness into his backpack, before slinging it over his shoulder.

They rode the elevator down to the main floor and to Evie's surprise, found themselves in the middle of downtown D.C. Nate reached in his backpack and produced two metro cards. Evie giggled her way through the entire trip, loving the fact that no one riding the metro knew they were riding with a dragon.

Now that they were walking up the stairs to her apartment

on the northeast side of the city, Evie felt the first stirrings of unease about showing Nate where she lived. Unease she quickly shook off. If he was the type to look down on her for her crappy place, that was his problem.

As they walked up the stairs it hit her then that she didn't even have her key. The asshole who'd kidnapped her had all her stuff, including her cell phone, purse and keys. Who knew what had become of her belongings by now? Probably sold or in the trash.

She knocked on the door of the apartment and listened carefully for any movement behind the door. Mimi must not be home.

"I have to get the spare key from my neighbor. It'll just take a second."

Nate followed her as she walked two doors down the hall and knocked on her neighbor's door. After a few minutes, Mrs. Abdi opened the door. The older lady, an immigrant from Somalia, had pretty much adopted Evie as soon as they'd moved in. She said Evie reminded her of her daughter and had quickly proven that to be true with her blunt observations about everything in Evie's life.

"Evie! What happened to you?"

"It's a long story. But I lost my keys so I need the spare."

"Of course. It's right here." She stared at Evie's oversized clothing and sock-clad feet but luckily handed over the spare key without any questions. But she did stick her head out of the door to stare blatantly at Nate.

Evie used the key to unlock her door and Nate followed her into the dark apartment. She picked up the flashlight she'd left on the entry table and turned it on.

"Um, the lights aren't working right now." She didn't look at him as she said it.

"Mimi? Are you here?" She called out several times and then walked to the small kitchen in the back. "I guess she must have gone out right after we talked on the phone."

When she turned around, Nate's eyes glittered in the semi-darkness. Even in the dark she could see the forbidding look on his face.

"Gather your things. We need to be ready to go when your mother arrives."

Evie's mouth dropped. "But then I won't get to spend any time with her. I need to make sure she's okay!"

Nate seemed to live a pretty solitary life so he probably

didn't understand her need to look after her mom. Even though she made bad choices and generally drove her crazy, she was still her mother. She couldn't be happy not knowing if Mimi was okay.

Nate crossed his arms. She was starting to recognize when he was about to go all alpha dragon on her but she wasn't backing down.

"That's not what I–"

They were interrupted by the front door crashing open followed by a soft curse. She pushed past Nate. Her mother lay sprawled on the floor.

"Evie! You're already here. I just had to go out for a few things." Judging by the smell, the only thing she'd had to go out for had been alcohol.

Shame was like hot needles in her throat. Evie took her mother's arm and helped her sit up against the wall. She pulled her heels off, having learned from experience that they were an accidental weapon on a drunk Mimi.

"Does she need medical care? I can smell the toxins in her system from here," Nate asked softly.

"She's just drunk," Evie murmured, thoroughly mortified.

Mimi looked up at the unfamiliar voice. When she saw Nate, she shrank back slightly. Evie patted her shoulder. She'd been planning to introduce the idea of a dragon boyfriend to her mother slowly but with Nate's slitted eyes on display, it was a little late for that.

"Is he one of them?" she whispered to Evie. Without waiting for an answer, she continued, "If I met a man like that… I wouldn't care if he had a tail either."

Behind her Nate laughed softly. Fortunately he didn't seem offended. Instead he knelt on the floor next to them and held out his hand.

"Hello, mother of my mate. I am Nathan Drake and I'm very pleased to meet you. Now let's get you up."

Nate lifted her mother from the ground easily and strode toward the kitchen. Evie trailed behind them, embarrassment warring with practicality. Part of her wished she'd asked him to wait for her outside so he wouldn't be forced to deal with this. What a first impression! However she had to admit his way of handling things was much faster than her usual process of coaxing Mimi to cooperate.

He set Mimi carefully in one of the chairs at the small kitchen table, then moved to the sink. After taking a glass from the cabinet above the sink, he filled it with water and brought it to the table.

"Thank you." Mimi beamed up at him.

She took several careful sips, somehow still managing to spill most of it on the tabletop and over the front of her dress. Nate, to his credit, didn't bat an eyelash.

Mimi glanced over at her. "He's a handsome one, I'll give you that. But handsome men can be trouble."

"No trouble will ever befall either of you, ever again. Your daughter is my greatest treasure. As her mother, you are precious to me also."

Evie could practically see her mother melt into a puddle right then and there. She could understand. Nate had a way of looking at a woman that made her feel like the most priceless of jewels.

Nate motioned toward the stairs. "Come now, *mi maaren tesarik*. You need rest."

"Oh, I'm fine–"

Nate picked her up, ignoring her protests. As he carried her down the hall, Evie pointed out which room belonged to her mother. Nate put her down on the bed gently and then left the room, pulling the door closed behind him. Grateful for his understanding, Evie managed to cajole her mother into a long t-shirt and then into bed. Evie stood for a moment just watching her sleep. With the covers pulled up to her neck, Mimi looked like a child.

Out in the hall, Nate leaned against the wall staring at his phone. He looked up when she left the room.

"Is she okay?"

"She's fine, she just needs to sleep it off."

"This changes things." Nate glanced behind her at the closed door. "She can't fly like that. So we will stay here tonight and then leave in the morning."

"Wait, Mimi is coming with us? I'm not sure that's a good idea. Your place is in the middle of nowhere. How would she get back home? I don't want you to have to fly her back again the next day."

He took her arm gently and led her to the other bedroom. She put the flashlight she carried down on the nightstand, turning it off to save the battery. Moonlight saved the room from complete darkness but she still wished she could see his expression.

After closing the door behind him, Nate asked "Why would she come back?"

"Um, because this is where we live?"

Nate started stripping off his clothes and it took all of Evie's concentration to remember what they were talking about.

"Neither of you will be coming back. You cannot stay here anymore."

"What?"

Shocked, she took a step back. Despite all the things he'd said to her, the idea that he actually wanted her to move in with him was crazy. Guys were usually trying to avoid having girls latch on to them, not encouraging it.

"Evie, surely you didn't think I'd leave you here alone and unprotected? As for your mother, you would never be happy leaving her behind. My clan owns plenty of land now. There is room for her to stay with us. She'll be protected there."

"You want to take care of her, too?" she whispered.

Nate smiled, as if pleased that she finally understood. "Of course. You are *drakaaren* now. This is our way."

Stunned, Evie allowed him to usher her into the bed. Once he seemed satisfied that she was comfortable, he pulled out his phone.

"Rest, *mi tesarik*. I have to call my brother." He winked at her and then put the phone to his ear.

Evie wasn't sure how long she sat there, just watching him. He was talking in that rhythmic language again, that sounded like nothing but consonants to her. But the last thought she had before she succumbed to sleep was that she finally knew what the word mate truly meant.

It meant she'd finally found where she belonged.

Nate pinched the bridge of his nose. His brother was bringing him up to date on a range of security issues, none of which made him feel any better that he couldn't get Evie and her mother to safety until the next morning.

He glanced behind him to the bed where his mate slumbered. *I'll make it safe for you,* he thought. Even if he had to swallow his pride and make peace with Avan. He would do it for the sake of his mate.

When Ian finally finished detailing the long list of things Kavan had threatened them with, Nate sighed.

"There's something I haven't told you, brother. Avan is coming after us so hard for this delivery because the cargo contained something more valuable than usual. Something dangerous."

"What?"

"A girl."

Ian cursed, a surprising sound coming from him. "The girl you had in your den. Your mate." He was quiet for a moment. "And you didn't tell me until now. Did you think I would betray you?"

Nate sucked in a shocked breath. Honor was a point of pride for them all, especially since their father's treachery had been why they'd lost their home, their name and their people. It hadn't even occurred to him that Ian would take his silence as a personal affront. He'd been thinking only with the distrustful mind of a dragon obsessed with his mate.

"No. I know you wouldn't do that. My only defense is that my mind was not right after I found her. It overwhelms me, this fear that she will be hurt or taken away."

Ian grunted. "I've heard stories that this is how it starts. That the mating fever makes even smart men stupid."

Relieved that his brother seemed to understand, Nate could only agree. "That's definitely how it feels."

"This changes things, Nate. It changes... everything. Do you think all of the deliveries we've done for him..."

"Yeah. It would explain all the weird rules. We've been participating in human trafficking and had no idea. No wonder he's always been so adamant that we're on time with each shipment."

"Fuck. This is going to give us some major blowback, you know that?"

"What would you have us do, Ian? I had no choice. I wasn't letting that bastard anywhere near Evie."

He'd forgotten to keep his voice down and Evie rolled toward him. He soothed her with a brush of his hand over her hair. She turned her face into his palm and whispered his name. The trusting gesture sent warmth through him, filling the cavity in the middle of his chest he would have sworn just twenty-four hours ago was completely empty.

"Of course not. I've always thought we needed to stand up to him. You're the rightful king, Nate. Not Avan or any of those other assholes he's sent after us. Maybe it's time we make him sweat a little."

"I have no interest in being King. All I want is for them to leave us alone."

"There might be something I can do about that. I need to check on something first. Just hang tight and I'll let you know."

"You're going out. Now?"

Ian chuckled. "Well, we don't all have someone to help us through the fever like you do. Lucky bastard. I'll be fine. Where I'm going the odds are pretty low that I'll run into any pretty girls. The damsels of the mountain are safe from me tonight."

That could only mean one thing. Ian was going back into Avan's territory.

"Be careful, brother."

"Always am. I look forward to meeting my new sister. Later. After you guys come up for air."

When he hung up he could still hear Ian's laughter.

He was glad someone could see the humor in the situation. All he could see was the possibility of war, which would mean certain death for their small clan. Hopefully his brother, the great negotiator, could find a way to bring an accord. It was time to come out of hiding. Evie deserved more than a life in the shadows.

"Nate?"

He pulled the covers back and got in bed next to her. "I'm sorry I woke you. Ian needed to tell me what to expect tomorrow."

"Expect?"

"There will be fallout from lying to the King. Ian wanted to warn me to be on guard. It's one of the reasons it's so important that we get you and your mother to safety as soon as possible. I want you on my land where we can protect you."

"Won't your brothers have an issue with you bringing on two extra people they have to protect?"

"My brothers have honor. We protect family and they would have it no other way."

She raised her hand to touch his face. "Nate, I just wanted you to know... I love you."

Emotions stormed through him and his heart soared. It

was the first time his mate had said the words to him and he'd treasure the memory of it always. Before he could push through the lump in his throat to respond, Evie continued.

"This is all so overwhelming. That you feel this way about me and that you want to take care of my mom. But I wanted you to know that."

When their lips met this time, Nate lost it. He was with his mate. She loved him. And he loved her more than life. All the desire of the mating fever hit him at once and he tugged the oversized sweatpants she was still wearing down. He'd never been so grateful that he slept nude since there was nothing in his way when he thrust into her. They froze in that position, absorbing the incredible pleasure of being one again.

"Nate. I love you so much."

Her cries only drove his insane need to possess her higher. He bent his knees, stabilizing himself to take her harder. Deeper. He'd be lucky if he got through the night without losing what was left of his sanity.

Evie's hand trailed over his shoulders and down to his ass. He growled low in his throat as she held on to the muscles, using them as leverage to encourage him to take her harder. Nate's hips swung freely, pinning her to the bed. She shivered and bucked beneath him, finally coming apart with a tortured cry.

He caught the sound with his mouth, sucking her tongue into his mouth. She whimpered and clutched at his back at the erotic action. Then he was the one at her mercy when she tightened around him, clamping down so hard he swore his dick would have bruises.

He let out a low moan and then planted one hand beneath her to steady him as he ground against her. It wasn't going to be long before he followed her into ecstasy. All it took was looking down to where they were joined and he growled out his pleasure. Evie held on to him while he came down, stroking over his back and neck.

Once he could breathe again, he rolled over and pulled her into the cradle of his arms. "I love you too, Evie. Now sleep. We have a long day ahead of us tomorrow."

8

Evie woke with a jolt.

It was much darker in the room than when she'd fallen asleep but she could still make out the familiar shapes of her dresser and the closet door across the room. She sat up slowly, unsure what had woken her. Nate slept next to her peacefully. Nothing seemed out of place.

Still, her heart was racing.

Evie took several deep breaths. She'd always been a light sleeper so it wasn't that surprising that she would have trouble sleeping tonight. It would take a pretty strong person not to be affected by the things that had happened to her over the past two days. She had every right to be a little wound up.

It wasn't every day a girl was claimed by a dragon.

Evie knew that she wouldn't be able to go right back to sleep so figured it was as good a time as any to check on Mimi. She padded to the door and opened it carefully, turning the knob slowly so the latch wouldn't catch. Nate had to be exhausted. The man deserved his rest after he flew her home, took such sweet care of her mother and then made love to her so vigorously.

Even though he had decided that he was her protector, she wanted to care for him, too. He called her his heart but she wanted to be more than that. She wanted to be his soft place to land and the one person who provided him solace from all his burdens.

She wanted to be his heaven.

It was brighter in Mimi's room, the light from an almost-full moon shining directly through her window. Mimi was all tangled up in the sheets so Evie pulled them gently to free her arms. Her mother came awake with a soft snort.

"It's just me. Go back to sleep."

But instead of going back to sleep Mimi sat up, her blonde

hair flying around her face. "I'm glad you're back, Evie. I was so worried."

Her mom sounded slightly more lucid than earlier. Evie wondered if she even remembered what had happened. As if sensing her thoughts, Mimi squeezed her hand.

"I hope I didn't embarrass you. It seems like I'm always doing that. I'm going to stop drinking so much, I promise."

Promises hurt worse, Evie knew. Because once upon a time she'd been naive enough to believe in them only to be disappointed.

"It's okay, Mimi. You just need to sleep it off."

"I know you don't believe me. But this time, I mean it. I'm going to make you proud of me." She let go of Evie's hand long enough to prop herself up with her pillow. "Your young man, he's a strange one."

Evie couldn't really argue with that. "Yeah, I guess he is. But then again, so am I."

Mimi patted her hand. "You're not strange. Just a dreamer. You would have gone far if you hadn't been saddled with taking care of me. You'd have a better life if I'd given you up."

"Oh Mimi. Don't say that."

"It's true. It was probably selfish to keep you but I'm not sorry. You've made me so happy every day, sweet girl. That's all I want for you. For you to be as happy as you've made me." Mimi yawned and closed her eyes.

Tears clogged her throat as she watched her mother nod off. Despite how many times she'd wondered what her life would have been like without the baggage her mother seemed to drag behind them, she couldn't imagine life without her. The woman who'd read her the same tattered picture book over and over because she knew Evie loved it. The woman who'd taken care of her when she was sick and kept every one of her childhood drawings as if they were precious art. For all her faults, Mimi had always loved her.

Evie stood carefully, trying not to rock the bed too much. Just as her hand landed on the doorknob, she heard her name.

"It's okay. You're at home now. You can sleep." She moved back to the bed and grabbed the hand Mimi held out. It wasn't unusual for her to wake several times in the night after drinking, usually disoriented and cranky.

"How did I get in bed?" Mimi looked around the room suspiciously.

"Nate carried you. Do you remember?"

Then Mimi smiled. "Oh yes. Your dragon man. Doesn't take no for an answer, does he? Is he always like that?"

"Yeah. Pretty much."

Mimi rolled over and buried her face in the pillow but Evie could still hear her mumbled, "*Lucky girl.*"

She left Mimi snoring softly and continued down the hall to the kitchen for a glass of water. As soon as she reached the sink, she pulled down a glass. The floor creaked behind her. Alarmed she tried to turn around, only to find herself yanked backward and the cold bite of steel against her throat.

The glass in her hand fell to the floor and shattered. The tinkling sound of glass breaking was almost as terrifying in the stillness as the knife.

"Scream and you die," a harsh voice whispered.

Evie trembled but managed to stop her shriek of terror. "Who are you? What do you want?"

"I'm the one who's going to slit your throat if you make a

sound. Don't get any bright ideas about screaming for your dragon boyfriend, either."

Evie gulped. If he knew about Nate, there was no telling what he was after. Maybe he thought he could extort the dragons for money or he could be one of the nut jobs who hunted them for their blood and talons. Either way, this wasn't going to end well.

"I'm not going to scream. I just want to know what you want from me. I don't have any money."

"Money isn't what I want. I'm here for you. You won't get away this time."

Get away this time? Her veins turned to ice. Oh god, no. The guy who had abducted her had come back to finish the job. How could she have been so stupid? Of course, he'd not only known exactly where to look since he'd had her wallet but he hadn't even had to break in since he had her keys, too.

"Okay, I'll go with you. I don't want anyone to get hurt."

To her surprise, the knife at her throat lowered slightly. "Despite what you think, I don't want anyone to get hurt either. I just want to save my brother."

Evie took a chance and turned slightly until she could see his face. "Save him from what?"

"Madness."

The stark answer told her nothing. If this guy got her outside and flew her somewhere else, there was no way Nate could track them down. If she was going to get out of this alive, she needed to stall him and hope that Nate finally noticed she wasn't in bed with him anymore.

"I really think you have the wrong person. There's nothing special about me. Literally nothing. I'm not exactly super-model material here. And I was a solid C student in school. Why would you think I could help your brother in any way?"

He gripped her tighter. "You smell so fertile and you're exactly his type. It's against everything we believe in to hurt a female but I had to get you to him. If there's any chance you could be the one, *I had to try.*"

He sounded so tortured that Evie didn't doubt that he was telling her the truth. No matter how crazy it all sounded to her, he believed what he was saying.

"The one for what?" she whispered.

But it seemed he was done with explanations. "Quiet. It's time for us to go. No more stalling."

Evie squeezed her eyes shut and thought of Nate.

Please, wake up. I need you.

Wake up. I need you.

Wake up. I need you.

WAKE UP.

Nate woke instantly as his scales came out. All his senses on alert, he took note of his surroundings quickly. He had excellent night vision so he was able to ascertain the most important things right away, namely that Evie wasn't in bed with him anymore.

Our mate is in danger.

His dragon itched to come out. Trusting his instincts, Nate got out of bed and pulled his jeans on quickly before opening the door. It was quiet. Too quiet. After looking in the other bedroom to make sure Evie wasn't in there, he continued down the hall. He stopped before he reached the kitchen when he heard footsteps far too heavy to be hers.

He turned the corner quickly, rage flowing through him when he saw the knife against her throat. The man behind her was an older version of the young boy he'd once played with in the mountains of their ancestral lands.

"Hello, cousin."

Jovan bared his fangs at him. "Hello, traitor."

Nate's talons came out. It was foolish to allow his cousin to bait him. He knew what his game was. Pride could force an untested warrior to show his hand too early but they were children no longer and so much more was at stake.

"This actually makes sense. That you're involved, I mean. I couldn't figure out why Avan would bother to hire a courier to ferry something illegal. But he isn't the one behind this, is he?"

Jovan didn't answer just continued edging around the perimeter of the kitchen, Evie scrambling to move with him. The glass on the floor shifted beneath their feet. He had to keep him talking long enough to figure out a plan. Because there was no way he could let him leave here with Evie. He'd never see her again.

"Is he really that close to dissolution that bringing him random women seemed like a good idea?"

"He's close enough. We had to do something," Jovan spat.

"So whose idea was it? Probably Kavan, right? He was always the manipulator. But he can't be away from the king for too long and we both know *you* aren't strong enough to carry a crate yourself."

Jovan scowled and flexed his stunted left arm. Physical disabilities were rare in shifters but they did happen. His arm had compromised his ability to fly even as a child.

"I guess we'll find out if I'm strong enough, won't we?"

Nate dropped his conciliatory act. "You know I will hunt you to the ends of the earth as long as you have my mate."

Jovan sniffed her hair, taking great pains to rub his face against her. Evie whimpered which sent his dragon into a fit. "She's unmarked."

"An oversight, I assure you. She's mine."

Jovan moved backward slightly, pulling Evie with him. "Which means you aren't going to do anything while I'm holding her. Your love for her ties your hands. You won't attack us as we're flying away either because if I drop her, she dies."

Nate wanted to roar with frustration. His cousin was right and they both knew it. Since he hadn't bitten her yet, Evie had none of the advanced healing or longevity that his venom would give her. He couldn't risk injuring her in a rescue attempt. Anything he did to save her could result in her death.

"Well, if I'm dying anyway," Evie said, right before she rammed her head back into Jovan's nose. Blood sprayed out as he staggered back, painting Evie's face and hair.

"You bitch!" he howled, clutching his face.

She ran to Nate and he pushed her behind him. Then he inhaled and roared fire, all at once thankful for the gifts his royal blood gave him. His cousin's screams rang out as his skin charred.

Jovan staggered and then fell. His eyebrows and hair were gone, replaced by open wounds. As they watched, the skin started healing. It was an excruciating process to heal such extensive injuries. Nate knew this from experience.

Keeping himself in front of Evie, he regarded the miserable wretch before him.

"You made a mistake coming after my mate, cousin. I was too young to challenge when you cast me out but I'm not a scared little *draakling* anymore. If I think for even a moment you're a threat to my queen, *I will end you* and the entire Rivenell clan. Go and tell that to your king."

Jovan tried to speak but all that came out was a garbled croak. He clutched his throat.

Behind him, Evie let out a choked sound. He understood why. The smell of charred flesh turned even his hardened stomach.

He motioned to the door. "I'm only allowing you to live so you can carry my message. Get the hell out before I change my mind."

Jovan staggered to his feet and then walked to the front door. Nate waited, unmoving, until he heard his cousin's footsteps fade away and then the distant beat of wings. In the quiet of night, the broken glass on the floor seemed even more ominous, like portents of what was to come. Is this what would happen to his clan after the war that had surely started tonight? Everyone he loved broken beyond repair?

Evie wrapped her arms around his waist and squeezed

lightly. He turned and kissed her forehead, drawing strength from having his mate near.

"I was so scared you wouldn't wake up in time."

He held her closer. There were no words that could express his terror on seeing her with a knife at her throat. Although he loved that she was so fierce and so brave as to take on a dragon to free herself, he'd be tortured for years by the many ways tonight could have gone differently.

"Don't ever take a chance like that again. He could have killed you."

Evie nodded. "I know. But since he kept talking about all the different ways I could die while he was kidnapping me, I figured I'd rather go here than by falling from the sky or something."

Nate grunted. While he understood her logic, they were going to have a long talk about putting her life in danger for any reason. He held her closer.

Tomorrow.

After a few minutes, she looked up at him with a mischievous gleam in her gorgeous eyes. "You know how I said I wasn't impressed by all the dragon stuff?"

"Yeah?"

Evie shrugged. "Well, the whole *touch my queen and I will end you* thing? Kind of impressive. Just a little bit."

In that moment, Nate did something he'd never expect after fighting a member of a rival clan and making a promise of war.

He laughed.

9

After the events of the prior night, Evie had thought she wouldn't sleep a wink but surprisingly, she'd slept quite soundly. Nate woke her early and waited patiently as she'd packed her favorite belongings and Mimi's in two small duffel bags.

She'd thought it would be a hard sell to convince Mimi to come with them but to her surprise, her mother decided that moving to dragon territory was a thrilling adventure. Mimi had embraced every step of their journey with enthusiasm and she'd loved the experience of flying just as much as Evie did.

Mimi let out a little whoop as they circled around and around, finally coming to a stop in front of Nate's den. Before they'd left the city, he'd secured their luggage together with special ropes so he could carry it in his talons. He'd promised to arrange for movers to pack up the apartment but Evie was tempted to tell him not to bother. It was time for a new start.

He dropped their bags first and then landed several feet away. Evie unhooked the harness and climbed down, Mimi scrambling down after her. When he didn't shift immediately, Evie realized with a startled giggle that he didn't want to shift in front of her mother. It seemed even dragons could be bashful sometimes.

"Um, Mimi. Can you turn around?"

"Why?" Her mother furrowed her brow.

"Because Nate needs to shift. And when he does, he'll be naked."

"Oh. Okay."

Mimi turned her back and immediately the air crackled with energy. Evie watched as the gold dragon in front of her shrank down and then Nate stood from a crouched position. She rushed forward and handed him his back-pack. He pulled out his jeans and stepped into them.

"It's okay to turn around now."

Her mom turned and then smiled when she saw Nate. "I have a feeling things will never be boring around here."

Nate laughed. "That's true. Let me show you where you'll be staying."

Over the next hour Evie helped get her mom settled into the guest cottage. It was a small replica of Nate's den, situated only a stone's throw away. Nate pointed out his brother's dens, arranged in a loose semi-circle around his. They had deliberately kept their residences close so they could guard each other.

Mimi finally pushed them out, claiming she was tired and needed a nap. But right before she closed the door, she winked at Evie.

"Well, my mom likes you," she told him as they walked back to his place.

Nate looked pleased. "I hope so. I want her to know that her daughter is in good hands."

Even though they'd just been together last night, desire sparked anew. Evie clutched his hand tighter. "Very good hands."

Nate groaned. "Stop that. I'm not touching you again until I've marked you properly. I didn't want to bite you until you understood what it meant. But by not marking you, I left you vulnerable to being claimed by another. We're fixing that right now."

When they arrived at his den, she saw that a dark-haired man that bore a striking resemblance to Nate waited for them. When they got closer, Nate pulled him into a hug. He turned to her, his eyes shining.

"Gavin, may I present to you Evangeline Ford. My mate and your future queen."

Evie's mouth went dry at the overly formal introduction. She waved weakly. "Um, hi?"

Gavin held out his hand and when she took it, raised it to his lips. "Greetings, my queen."

This is too much, Evie thought.

"Okay, enough of that. My dragon can't handle it until I have my mark on her." Nate pushed himself between them. "Where the hell is Ian?"

Gavin shrugged. "He left yesterday and never came back. Probably knee deep in some...." His eyes cut over to Evie and then his cheeks flushed red. "Some fine female company."

She stifled a laugh. Nate growled.

"We're going forward with the claiming. I'm not waiting anymore. The old laws only require one witness, anyway."

Nate led them into his den and closed the door once they were all inside. He took her hand and kissed it, the same way his brother had. But this time, Evie almost melted into a puddle right there on the floor.

"I'm going to mark you now, my heart. Do you understand what that means?"

She nodded. "You have to bite me. Will it hurt?"

"Only for a second. My venom will numb the area and then you won't feel anything. But I'm more concerned about whether you're prepared for what being my mate forever means. There's no turning back after this. If you leave me, I'll waste away pining for you. There is no divorce in dragon culture. There's only eternity. Are you ready for that?"

Evie took a moment to truly examine her heart. So much had happened so quickly and she knew to an outsider it would all seem like insanity. But she knew her heart and what it wanted.

"Yes, I'm ready."

He kissed her softly. "Turn around."

She glanced uncertainly at Gavin, who looked as uncomfortable as she felt.

"Um, Nate? Why do we need an audience?"

He brushed her hair over her shoulder, baring her neck. "You only need witnesses to the mate claim when a regent takes a mate. I'm stepping up to the throne. War is coming and we need to be ready."

Evie was suddenly filled with fierce purpose. It was insane to think that fate had brought her here just for this moment but she'd never been so sure that she was exactly where she was meant to be before.

"I'm with you until the end. Do it."

She hissed at the searing pain in her neck but it quickly dulled into an achy throb. Time suspended and she sagged against Nate. Her hand sank into his thick hair, holding him against her neck. All her sensations were suddenly magnified, like the press of his hard frame against her back and the wet glide of his lips against her neck. When he finally pulled away, long moments later, she was boneless and aching for an entirely different reason.

"Now, we're together forever," Nate whispered against her neck.

It turned out that biting your mate didn't help soothe the mating frenzy at all. As Nate soon learned, having his venom in his beloved's neck only made the obsession worse. He'd be lucky if his brother ever spoke to him again after the unceremonious way he'd kicked him out after the claiming ceremony.

At least Gavin had been laughing. Nate had been completely consumed with getting inside his mate. Even after making love to her twice, it still wasn't enough. Which was why he couldn't believe someone was stupid enough to interrupt him now.

"Just ignore it," Evie pleaded. Her teeth latched on to his earlobe and he let out a growl. "They'll go away if we don't answer."

The knock at his front door only got louder.

"Damn it all to the seven hells!" Nate pulled back from her warm embrace and stormed to the front door. He yanked it open. "What the hell do you want?"

Jonas shrank back from the doorway. Then he put his hand over his younger brother's eyes. "Sorry, sir. But I had to come. It's about Ian."

"Hold on." He turned around and then walked back to his room. His jeans were crumpled at the end of the bed but he had to search through his dresser for a shirt. Sensing his urgency, Evie quickly dressed as well.

When they came out, Jonas and Sam were sitting in his living room. He'd had only limited interaction with Sam. He wasn't sure if there was a difficulty with his voice or if it was psychological but from what he'd observed, the boy only communicated with his older brother. At least as far as Nate had seen.

"Now, what's this about Ian?"

Jonas glanced over at his brother, who nodded emphatically. "Sam and I were out scouting earlier. We went a little further than usual. Ian was flying over us so it didn't seem that risky. I think he was on his way back here."

Sam tugged at his sleeve urgently.

"I'm getting to that part." Jonas looked back at them. "I didn't see it, but Sam says he saw it happen. He saw Ian fall."

Nate glanced between them uncertainly. He didn't want to question the young man's integrity but it was hard to believe their story. Ian was an experienced flyer and even more adept at maneuvering in the air than Nate was. It was lunacy to imagine his brother felled by anything.

"You saw him fall. Did you see what hit him?" He addressed Sam directly. It seemed rude not to. But the boy shrank into himself and hid behind Jonas.

"Sorry. He only talks to me. But I already asked him that. That's what's so weird, you see. He says Ian wasn't hit by anything. He just fell from the sky for no reason at all."

Nate wanted to disregard their claims. It would be easier to ignore it as childish pranks and go back to mating his gorgeous queen. But something deep inside him accepted what they were saying as truth. He pulled out his phone and texted Gavin. Five minutes later, his brother walked in.

Sam shrank even more if that was possible, until he was practically burrowed into the couch cushions.

"I came as soon as I got your text. What do you think happened?"

Nate hated to even voice it aloud but coming a day after

his fight with Jovan, it was impossible to ignore the implications.

"If Ian was felled, it wasn't an accident. He was attacked. You know what this means. It's time."

Gavin bowed. "So it will be done."

Evie watched with wide eyes as Jonas and Sam followed Gavin outside.

"What will be done?"

He pulled her into his arms. "We are at war with Rivenell. Officially."

She rested her head against his chest. "Your brothers are going to hate me. None of this would be happening if you hadn't had to protect me."

Nate grasped her head gently, cradling her face in his palms. It took a few minutes before she met his gaze and when she did, her beautiful dark eyes were lit with sorrow and regret.

"They won't blame you. I was protecting my mate. They understand that."

She shook her head. "How can they understand something that puts them all at risk?"

"Because they know what taking a mate means. They understand that you are what holds me together. Without you I am but skin and blood and bone. I exist but I don't live. I breathe but I don't feel. You are the heart of a king, Evangeline Drake. Never forget that."

He kissed her softly, gratified when she leaned up on her toes to kiss him back.

"I'm counting on you to remind me. Forever."

Ian Drake rolled over and tried to breathe through the scent of death. His mind was churning and even in that state, he knew that something wasn't right. He was in danger. He tried to shift and felt terror unlike anything he'd ever known when nothing happened.

He was completely defenseless.

Then in the midst of the chaos in his mind, he smelled something perfect and right. A feminine fragrance that reminded him of sunlight and gold and blue skies. Something that was his alone. His dragon rumbled approvingly.

My mate. Mi tesarik.

A soft hand landed on his mouth, bringing the sweet fragrance closer. "Please, you have to be quiet. Your life depends on it."

He opened his eyes briefly and beheld the face of his angel.

Then a moment later, all was dark.

I hope you enjoyed *Nathan's Heart*. Join my VIP list to find out more about the series and get FREE books from me!

Are you a fan of **really** inappropriate romantic comedy? Find out what happens when a hotshot ad executive discovers his rooster will only crow for one woman. His competition. **One-click BEG ME now!**

OR

Keep reading for a special excerpt of Ian's book.

***Ian's Fall* is available now!**
mmalonebooks.com/iansfall

When Ian Drake is shot down after visiting dragon territory, his only thought is to warn his brothers of the coming danger. Attacked with some kind of chemical weapon, he is unable to shift into his dragon form. For the first time in years, the protector finds himself vulnerable and his salvation comes in a form he'd never expect. A woman.

As Ian Drake flew lower and prepared to shift, he observed his land with pride. The mountains spread out below him like a feast, bursting with the first colors of spring. Although it wasn't *his* exactly, he felt a sense of ownership over these mountains after they had served as his refuge for so many years. A refuge that he and his brothers had sorely needed.

After their parents had been executed for treason, they'd been cast out of their ancestral lands. In the blink of an eye, they had gone from the spoiled princes of Rivenell, one of the mightiest dragon clans in the world, to destitute outsiders. His oldest brother had kept them together and somehow managed to find work so they wouldn't starve. Other the years, they'd managed to build a thriving business locating and retrieving priceless objects for some of the world's most influential people.

Although they'd managed to build their own small clan, Ian still yearned for the chance to make things right. His older brother was the rightful king and even though Nate didn't seem to care, Ian wanted him on the throne. His desire to see justice done had pushed him into riskier and riskier behaviors over the past few years. But what he'd just done was up there.

If he'd been in his human skin, he would have grinned imagining his cousin Avan's reaction when he discovered the former regent's royal seal carved into every rock, tree and hill that Ian had been able to find. Each branch of the royal family in Rivenell had their own crest. It had been years since his father's mark had been seen and Ian knew it would send a strong message.

Despite what Avan thought, there were still dragons who supported the restoration of the rightful king to the throne. If they could organize them, there was a chance they could overtake Avan and the current regime.

A whistle caught his ear. Two figures waved from below. He recognized Jonas and Sam, the young boys his brother Gavin had taken on as apprentices. Ian let out a roar of acknowledgment. Distrustful of humans in general, Ian had thought it was a foolish move to allow humans into their small clan at first. But he'd eventually had to admit that taking on some help was a good idea.

It turned out that the two brothers actually had some dragon heritage but couldn't shift. Nulls were rare in the dragon community and weren't generally treated any better than humans. But despite his defect, Jonas had proven himself an asset many times over. He handled all their dealings with the local humans. Everyone mainly gave them a wide berth but it helped to have someone non-threatening to deal with the locals.

Keeping the peace with the humans was a delicate balance

between fear and mutual respect. Something he wasn't good at. He tended toward aggression first and conciliation second. As his brother's right hand, it was his job to watch his back and keep their little clan safe. Being the regent's second in a small clan was no less difficult than in a big clan. Probably more so because they had fewer resources to work with. The fact that he was currently on a mission during Mating Fever proved that fact. He should be locked in his den working off the fever with a willing female.

Ian grunted, the sound coming out on a bark of fire. Once he got back to his den maybe he would put in a call to one of the local women. There were always humans fascinated by dragon males so he never had trouble finding female company. But despite the fire burning through his system, the thought held little appeal. As the years passed, it was harder and harder to work up the enthusiasm to entertain a human woman who just wanted the chance to say she'd ridden a dragon. Now that his older brother had found his one true mate, the secret yearning to find something real was stronger than ever.

Something flew by his ear and Ian flinched. The motion put him off course and that's probably the only reason he saw the dart fly past. The dart that would have hit him if he hadn't moved. Ducking into a twist and roll motion, Ian streaked through the sky. He'd been flying almost as long as he'd been walking and after a lifetime of flying with his brothers was particularly skilled at evading capture.

His mind raced as he flew lower and darted through the trees. Had someone seen what he was doing in Rivenell last night? Why wait until now to follow him? More importantly, where the hell was he going to go?

The last thing he wanted was to lead them to his land. If there had been time to warn his brothers of what was coming perhaps but he'd die before he led trouble to their door while they lay unsuspecting.

Something flew right by his face. His ears registered the sound right before pain exploded everywhere.

Ian was aware of himself falling but all of his focus was on pulling air into the lungs that currently felt like they were on fire. Bones popped and stretched as he shifted. He passed out and then woke as he shifted again, the process completely out of his control.

Aware suddenly of how fast he was falling, he stretched his wings trying to slow his descent. It was a struggle to get his limbs to respond, like they were attached to his body but outside of his control somehow. The world around him was a blur of blue, green and orange as he streaked through the sky falling end over end. The trees below him rushed up to meet him.

He had to shift. His scales would protect him somewhat and he'd sustain far fewer injuries in his dragon form. But as he concentrated with all of his focus, the part of him that was dragon was completely silent. It was like he was alone in his body for the first time since he'd shifted as a child. His dragon wasn't going to be able to save him this time.

As the ground got closer all he could think was, *This is going to hurt.*

***Ian's Fall* is available now!**
mmalonebooks.com/iansfall

Have you read the other **MATING FEVER** books yet?

DRAGON SHIFTERS

- *Minx Malone*

Nathan's Heart, Brotherhood of Bandits

- *Saranna DeWylde*

Ondrej, Drago Knights MC

- *Ronin Winters*

Mica, Dragon Horde

- *Elsa Jade*

Dragon Fever, Masters of the Flame

BEAR SHIFTERS

- *V. Vaughn*

Andre, Rocked by the Bear

- *Elle Thorne*

Cross, Barely After Dark

- *Kenzie Cox*

Cyrus, Black Bear Outlaws

- *Selene Charles*

Chance, Bears of Kodiak

Check out www.thematingseason.com to keep up to date!

DO YOU READ CONTEMPORARY ROMANCE?

If so, let me introduce you to the Alexander brothers...

BEING A GOOD GIRL ISN'T ALL IT'S CRACKED UP TO BE...

Ridley attracts nothing but bad guys. Like "won't stop calling and then shows up in the bushes outside your house" type of guys.

So when she's confused for her twin while hiding out from her latest mistake, for once she decides to do the "wrong" thing.

BEING TALENTED ISN'T ALL IT'S CRACKED UP TO BE...

Jackson Alexander was born with the voice of an angel. But after his wife's death, he lost his will to sing. Or to love.

There's something about Ri that makes him want to try again. But when her lies are revealed, he has to make a choice. Trust her or his heart which just might break for good this time.

One More Day is available now at
mmalonebooks.com/onemoreday

EXCERPT OF ONE MORE DAY

Ridley yawned so widely it felt like the sides of her face might crack. The clock on the wall to her left told her it was almost two in the morning. She thought of the soft, decadent bed upstairs in the guest room she was using and almost whimpered. It was way past time for her to go upstairs and get some sleep.

Instead she turned her head and looked at Jackson again.

He was such a puzzle. Men who looked like him weren't

nice for no reason, yet he hadn't asked her for anything. He'd just been there when she had no one else. Why, she couldn't even begin to guess.

His features were relaxed in sleep, the long, sharp blade of his nose more prominent now that it didn't have to compete with his killer smile. His lashes rested against the tops of his cheekbones and she had to resist the urge to run a hand over his curly hair. It wasn't fair that he looked so beautiful and guileless in sleep when he carried such a lethal sexiness when fully awake.

"I would say 'penny for your thoughts' but I have a feeling *that* thought would cost more than I'm worth."

Ridley ripped her gaze from the curve of his lips up to his now wide-open eyes.

Oops.

"Hi. I was just..." She decided not to even address her blatant staring. "...wondering if I could borrow something to sleep in?"

"Sure, sure. Of course." He got up slowly, unfolding his long legs from the couch one at a time. "Follow me. Sorry I conked out at the end there. I guess I was more tired than I thought." He waved for her to follow him up the stairs and she did, keeping her eyes on her own feet so she couldn't ogle the way his jeans fit him as he walked.

She was in his room before she'd realized what she'd done. "Oh, I'll just wait out in the hall," she stammered.

"No. Stay." Those two simple words halted her in her tracks. He smiled a slow, sexy grin before pulling open the second drawer in his bureau. He rummaged for a while, pulling out shirts and then pushing them back in. "I'm trying to find one of my shorter ones so it won't swallow you up."

"Oh, I like them longer. It'll hang lower and cover my legs like a nightgown."

He stopped digging and glanced at her. Then his eyes dipped lower to take in her bare legs exposed by the mid-thigh, terry-cloth shorts she wore. "Right."

He held out a shirt and Ridley took it carefully, making sure their fingers didn't touch.

"Well, thanks again. Good night." She fled the room, racing down the darkened hallway, not stopping until she reached the door of the guest room. She turned the handle and opened the door, but before she entered she looked back.

She *had* to.

Jackson stood in the same position next to his dresser. The heat of his gaze burned over her entire body and she shivered as her nipples peaked against her shirt. She didn't know him well enough to interpret the look on his face but she could interpret her body's response.

God, she wanted him.

He'd been nothing but a gentleman all day, seeing to her every need, listening to her vent and keeping her company. He hadn't made any moves on her, hadn't done anything suggestive or said anything provocative. Was he just being a good host and making sure she made it to her room?

Or was he imagining what she would look like when she stripped off her clothes and went to bed wearing nothing but his shirt?

Jackson wasn't sure who moved first, but a second later he was down the hall and Ridley was in his arms. Her hair flowed over them as he held her against the wall. He buried his face in her neck and inhaled, his libido instantly going haywire at the warm, seductive scent of her skin. There were no words spoken between them, just the unspoken desires in their eyes.

I want you.

I know.

I want you, too.

When he finally anchored a hand in her hair and tilted her face up for his kiss, it was both a pain and a relief. Her lips opened under his with a breathy little moan. He would kick himself later for his angry assault on her mouth. There was no gentleness, no finesse. He held her captive against him as he took her mouth, capturing her tongue and sliding it against his own.

She was warm and soft in his arms, her breasts pressing against his chest as he held her against him. He was holding her too tightly but she didn't push away. She clung to him, her long legs snaking around his waist to hold him in the cradle of her thighs.

"Jackson," she pleaded.

"Hold on, baby. Just wait."

He groaned as she arched in his arms, rubbing her core

against him. She was perfect, so soft and responsive. He worked her, angling so he could rub right against her sweet spot. Damn if she didn't catch his rhythm right away, rocking her hips up as he ground against her.

"Jackson. Please, please, please—" She broke off with a strangled cry when he slid her down so she was riding his thigh.

She went rigid in his arms before her head fell back against the wall. Her eyelids drifted down as she shuddered beneath him.

"Oh yeah, that's it," he whispered.

That look. Damn if she wasn't the most beautiful thing he'd ever seen with her head thrown back, ecstasy all over her face as her most intimate muscles clenched against his thigh.

He'd be seeing that look in his dreams.

"I'm sorry. I'm so sorry," he gasped, then took her mouth in another crushing kiss, kissing her deeply until he again had to pull away just to breathe.

He ripped his mouth from hers, the sight of her swollen lips almost making him dizzy.

"I told myself I wasn't going to do this. You need someone to lend a helping hand, not take advantage." He pressed his forehead against hers and took a deep breath.

It should have been better when he couldn't see the way she looked up at him, so soft and trusting. But even with his eyes closed, he could still see her face. The way she looked at him made him feel powerless. He could literally feel his self-control oozing out, drop by drop.

"Oh, that's right. You're supposed to stay away from me. I'm a vulture, remember?" She licked his bottom lip and he groaned.

When she kissed a trail from his jaw down to his neck, he flinched and set her down. "That was my brother talking. I know better. But that doesn't make this a good idea."

"You really are a nice guy, aren't you?"

"Unfortunately, yes," he grumbled.

"Well, the fact that you don't seem any happier about it than I do..." She stood on tiptoe and wrapped her arms around his neck, brushing her body against his, inch by inch. "...makes me feel a little better. My ego anyway."

He stopped thinking the instant she plastered herself

against him. It took a moment for him to direct enough blood to his brain to translate what she was saying.

"I'm definitely not happy about it, beautiful. I'm just trying not to be what you think I am."

She pulled back and looked him in the eye. "Jackson—"

He cut her off before she could continue. "I have a family picnic tomorrow, so there's going to be a lot of people around. But we always have tons of food and good music. You're welcome to join us. I want you to make yourself at home while you're here."

It was asking for trouble, but he couldn't stop himself from taking another kiss, bending her back over his arm until she was forced to cling to his shoulders to stay on her feet. Then, while she was still dazed, he turned and walked off.

There was a cold shower calling his name.

ALSO BY MINX MALONE

- PARANORMAL ROMANCE -

Brotherhood Of Bandits

Nathan's Heart / Ian's Fall / Gavin's Curse

- ROMANTIC COMEDY -

BEG ME : My cock a doodle doo is on strike. Yeah I know, I can't believe it either. But he'll only crow for one woman. Spoiler Alert *she hates me*

ASK ME : Am I arrogant? Maybe. Do women still want me? Abso-F'ing-lutely. Then I meet the one woman who isn't impressed.

- CONTEMPORARY ROMANCE -

The Alexanders

One More Day : "Good girl" Ridley has always attracted bad guys. Now she's on the run and has nowhere to hide. So when

Jackson Alexander mistakes her for her twin, she decides to do something she knows is wrong. *She lies.*

The Things I Do for You : Nicholas Alexander finally has something the woman of his dreams needs. He'll give Raina a baby if she gives him what he wants. *Her*.

He's the Man : Matt Simmons is over Army doctors poking him until he sees his old babysitter, now a physical therapist, is h-o-t. Suddenly he's seeing the benefits of therapy.

Christmas with The Alexanders: The only gift Kaylee wants is for Elliott Alexander to stop treating her like she's invisible. When her car skids out of control on Christmas Eve, she's forced to reach out to the only man she trusts to save her.

VIP list exclusive!

All I Need is You : When the man she loves leaves town after their steamy kiss, Kaylee Wilhelm is done. But when she's targeted by a stalker, Eli is the only one who can protect her.

Say You Will : Mara Simmons has always known Trent Townsend is *The One*. But when she suspects his frequent business trips have *nothing* to do with business, she sets in motion a chain of events bigger than she can imagine and discovers that the man she loves just might be a stranger.

Just One Thing : Scientist Bennett Alexander is a bona fide genius but he still can't figure out how to "get the girl". So he hires a dating tutor. What could go wrong? Other than falling for his teacher, of course.

Bad King: My parents just put a gold diggers target on my back. But if all they want is a wedding, I can do that. I'll find the fiancee of their nightmares. *Who Wants to Marry a Billionaire? Must be completely inappropriate.*

Bad Blood : I'd do anything for my best friend's little sister. Until she asks for the one thing I can't give. One night. No rules. ***2019 RITA® Award Winner!***

Blue-Collar Billionaires

Inheriting billions from the deadbeat dad they never knew sounds pretty sweet. Until they find out what he really wants in exchange.

TANK / FINN / GABE / ZACK / LUKE

- ROMANTIC SUSPENSE -

(Co-authored with Nana Malone)

- The Shameless Trilogy
- The Force Duet
- The Deep Duet
- The Sin Duet
- The Brazen Duet

ABOUT THE AUTHOR

Minx Malone is a 2019 RITA® Award winner and a NYT & USA Today Bestselling author of completely inappropriate romantic comedy. She spends most days wearing Wonder Woman leggings and T-shirts that she's embarrassed for anyone to see while she plays with her imaginary friends.

She lives with her husband and their two sons in the picturesque mountains of Northern Virginia even though she is afraid of insects, birds, butterflies and other humans.

She also holds a Master's degree in Business from a prestigious college that would no doubt be scandalized at how she's using her expensive education.

facebook.com/minxmalone

twitter.com/minxmalone

instagram.com/minxmalone

bookbub.com/authors/m-malone

Printed in Poland
by Amazon Fulfillment
Poland Sp. z o.o., Wrocław

64568872R00096